SCAMMED

SCAMMED

Ron Chudley

VICTORIA • VANCOUVER • CALGARY

Copyright © 2009 Ron Chudley

All rights reserved. No part of this publication may be reproduced, stored in a retrieval system, or transmitted in any form or by any means—electronic, mechanical, audio recording, or otherwise—without the written permission of the publisher or a photocopying licence from Access Copyright, Toronto, Canada.

TouchWood Editions
#108 – 17665 66A Avenue
Surrey, BC V3S 2A7
www.touchwoodeditions.com

TouchWood Editions
PO Box 468
Custer, WA
98240-0468

Library and Archives Canada Cataloguing in Publication
Chudley, Ron, 1937-
Scammed / Ron Chudley.

ISBN 978-1-894898-88-1
I. Title.

PS8555.H83S24 2009 C813'.54 C2008-907719-9

Library of Congress Control Number: 2008942362

Edited by Marlyn Horsdal
Proofread by Christine Savage
Interior layout by Duncan Turner
Front cover photo by Yungshu Chao / istockphoto.com

Printed in Canada

TouchWood Editions acknowledges the financial support for its publishing program from the Government of Canada through the Book Publishing Industry Development Program (BPIDP), Canada Council for the Arts, and the province of British Columbia through the British Columbia Arts Council and the Book Publishing Tax Credit.

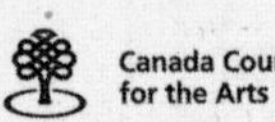

Conseil des Arts
du Canada

This book has been produced on 100% post-consumer recycled paper, processed chlorine free, and printed with vegetable-based dyes.

For my sons, Hugh and Ben.

PROLOGUE

The phone rang at 9:30 AM, half an hour after the man had gone to work. That was a good thing, since his wife discovered that the call involved financial matters, and her husband hated to waste time and creative energy on such dull stuff: what he called business gobbledygook. The cultured phone voice greeted her politely, checked her identity carefully, then gravely stated his business.

"This is William Fitzherbert. I am Inspector of Accounts for Inter Island Trust, where you are a valued customer. I'm phoning to give you a very serious warning."

"Goodness, Mr. Fitzherbert. What have I done?"

"No, no, I'm sorry," Fitzherbert said hastily. "You've done nothing wrong. This is a warning about a serious danger to your account."

But he would not tell her the problem immediately. As a protection for herself, and proof of his authenticity, he gave her a phone number, urging her to call back immediately. When she dialed, a businesslike woman's voice said, "Inter Island Trust Crisis Centre." Mentioning her call from Mr. Fitzherbert, she was put through immediately. "Thank you, Mrs. Lothian," Fitzherbert said. "Now you have proof of who I am and we can proceed. If all of our customers are as prompt as you, we'll foil these criminals."

"Oh, dear," she said breathlessly. "What criminals? What's going on?"

Frankly and concisely, he told her. Hackers had broken into the bank's main computer during the night, stealing a vast amount of customer information: account numbers, passwords and security codes. To prevent the thieves from plundering these accounts, it was vital that they be frozen immediately. To expedite matters, the crisis centre needed details of customers' codes and passwords so that their accounts could be protected. She was told not to worry: as soon as the necessary information was provided, her account would be secured. But, since the crisis centre had a huge job on their hands, working to protect all their customers, she was urged to be quick.

Flustered, feeling shocked, excited and not a little self-important, the woman did as she was bid. It was lucky, she thought. Had it been her husband who'd taken the call, he'd have fumed and argued, as he always did, wasting valuable time. Neither of them was any great shakes with finances, but at least she didn't feel that these things were beneath her. If it hadn't been for her, after all, they probably wouldn't even have the savings she was now helping to protect. So, when she'd provided the requested information, she felt not only relieved but quite proud.

The last thing that the thoughtful Mr. Fitzherbert did was make a polite request. Luckily, she was one of the first to be protected, but since it was going to take a considerable effort to contact everyone, she'd be doing her fellow customers a service if she didn't take up any more of the bank's time till the task was done. Also, so as not to start a panic, she was asked to keep this matter to herself. Could she hold out for a few days without accessing her account? Good. Next week she should visit her branch, set up a new password, and everything would be as before: crisis averted and no damage done. With a quiet sincerity that made the woman feel relieved and safe, Mr. Fitzherbert thanked her and wished her a good day.

After some thought, she concluded it was best not to bother her husband with the tale of their narrow escape. No matter that the crisis had been dealt with, just hearing about it would make him furious; when confronted by things he considered trivial—meaning just about everything outside his own interests—her husband could make life very difficult.

Her children were grown and important and a long way away. They were not easy to talk to, and the family dynamics were difficult enough as it was. So she decided to say nothing to anyone. She'd done her duty and that was enough.

In the following days, even with the bother of having to do without her bank card—she had to put some things, including food, on VISA, which she loathed—she continued to feel relieved and fortunate. If it hadn't been for the prompt action of Mr. Fitzherbert, where on Earth would they have ended up? This feeling lasted right up to the morning when, finally, she visited her branch of Inter Island Trust.

"You must have been terribly busy," she said to the nice girl at the wicket. "Is the trouble over? I hope I'm not bothering you too soon."

It was only when the puzzled cashier took her card and checked her account that the bleak truth emerged: the cupboard was bare. Upward of twenty thousand dollars had vanished into thin air.

ONE

In the accountancy business, April is a month of mayhem. As the income tax deadline approaches, life rises to a pitch of barely concealed hysteria. Even the advent of electronic filing seems to have made little difference. People simply wait that much longer to deliver their bundles of receipts, expecting harried accountants to decipher, calculate and wrestle them into acceptable scenarios and deliver them miraculously into the ether on time.

Greg Lothian was long past surprise at this state of affairs. After fifteen years as an accountant, a person would have to be brain-damaged to expect otherwise. Of course, his orderly mind still marvelled at the messiness of his clients' lives, but the end-of-year workload didn't bother him. He liked nothing better than to be alone with his calculator and computer, turning chaos into safe and sensible order. Since wrangling numbers gave him the kind of satisfaction that others derived from playing sports or watching TV, the occupation—and the overtime hours he accumulated—suited him very well. For Greg, April was usually a pleasant time, so it was with annoyance as well as dismay that he watched this one turn into disaster.

Right at the start he did something unbelievably foolish: stopping for gas on a weekend trip from his home in Victoria up-island to Nanaimo, he somehow left his wallet behind. Minutes later he realized the blunder and hurried back, but the precious article had vanished.

The counter clerk didn't have it. No one had seen it, which meant it must have become the reward for some low-life. The Nanaimo trip had to be nixed. Greg drove straight home—minus his driver's licence, which made him queasy—and got on the phone immediately, cancelling his credit cards. It was Monday morning before he could warn his bank. Then he lost another valuable hour replacing his licence.

Arriving home that evening, he met with yet another vexation: a notice reminding him that the lease on his apartment was due for renewal and announcing a substantial rent increase. No matter that the old charge had been very reasonable and that the new one wouldn't exactly break him; Greg was annoyed. All the more so because, other than going through the bother of finding new accommodation, there was nothing he could do about it.

Then, on April 28, just as activity at the office was nearing a climax, came the news about his father. The tyrannical old man, whom Greg had not seen since a blow-up at Christmas, had somehow managed to break his hip. But what was truly embarrassing was the way Greg found out: his mother phoned his sister in Vancouver, but didn't call him, telling Jill that she didn't want to bother her son at his busy time of the year. Needless to say, Jill had called immediately, tearing a strip off him, as if being kept in the dark had been his idea. In fact, neither of them found their parents easy to understand, let alone cope with, so pretending that he had received special favour in not being told about his dad was ludicrous. Naturally he'd do everything he could to help, Greg told his sister. What did she think?

As soon as he'd dealt with Jill, he called his mother, trying not to show his frustration. She hadn't meant to set his sibling on him, he knew. She was just always trying to placate everyone, which was why she'd never been able to stand up to the old man. "Hi, Mum, I just heard from Jill what happened. I'm sorry. How is Dad?"

"Oh, as well as can be expected. Thank you for calling, dear."

"Well, of course I'm calling! Mum, just because I'm busy doesn't mean . . . Never mind. About Dad—did he fall?"

"Yes, but it was something that should never . . ." his mother began, then broke off.

Greg realized she was crying. "Come on, Mum, don't worry. It's just his hip, isn't it?"

"Yes."

"They fix stuff like that all the time. It's routine. Dad'll be hopping about again in no time."

"I know, dear. That's not really why I'm upset."

"Then what's the matter?"

"It's about what caused it to happen. You see, he got in this awful rage, because of something stupid I did."

"Mum, Dad's been blowing his top ever since I can remember. You shouldn't blame yourself."

She sighed bitterly. "This time it truly was my fault."

How often had he heard that tune? Whatever displeased Walter Lothian was always held to be someone else's fault, and his wife had bought into that fiction from the beginning. What she was, Greg had belatedly come to understand, was an ego enabler, not only worshipping her husband and his paintings, but taking personal responsibility for anything that might intrude upon his precious creative process. "Okay, Mum, if you say so," he said. Then, changing the subject, "So—where is he, Cowichan District Hospital?"

"No, dear. Victoria General."

"Really? Why did they bring him all the way down here?"

"I don't know. Something about waiting times, I think. They're going to operate in the morning."

Greg was in his apartment. At this time in the evening, it wouldn't take more than twenty minutes to reach the local hospital. "Well, since he's down here, it's not too late for me to go and see him."

"That's sweet of you, dear," his mother replied, "but I don't think there'd be much point tonight."

"Why?"

"He's quite heavily sedated. That's why I left him and came back home. Tomorrow I'm going in first thing. The doctor said they'll need to put in pins when they set the hip, but it's supposed to be all over by noon. Why don't you come in the afternoon? He'll be awake then, and I'm sure he'd like to see you."

Greg felt frustrated all over again. Had she already forgotten why she hadn't called him in the first place? From now till midnight the day after tomorrow, he would barely have time to go to the bathroom. His parents had little respect for Greg's mundane occupation. His mother never admitted it, but his dad had always made his feelings abundantly clear: Greg's lack of artistic talent was a family embarrassment. Though that had never prevented them from using him as a tame tax accountant. "I'm afraid I'm badly tied up tomorrow," he said patiently. "Tax time—remember?"

"Oh, yes—you're a busy man, I know."

That reminded him of something he'd been intending to call her about; the packet of receipts and T4 forms she usually mailed him hadn't arrived, meaning he was going to be late filing their taxes. Since they usually got a rebate these days, it hardly mattered. The carelessness bothered him, but now didn't seem the time to bring it up.

"Daddy will be probably home in a couple of days," his mother was saying. "So don't you worry. When you have time, perhaps you can come up and visit him here."

She didn't say "finally," but then she wouldn't. She was so used to heavy scenes with Walter, she'd probably forgotten the one at Christmas that had made him so angry. He'd been putting off seeing his father ever since, and now, with the old man in hospital, he was irritated to find himself feeling guilty. "All right, Mum," he said abruptly. "I'm on my way."

"What, dear?"

"Tonight! I'll go see Dad tonight."

"But I told you—he's . . ."

"Mum, we both know it takes a lot more than sedation to shut him up for long. If he's awake, I can—I don't know—wish him luck or something. If not, at least you'll know I tried."

Ten minutes later he was in his Prius, driving north out of town. At 7:30 PM, the sky was clear, with a hint of afterglow over the Sooke Hills. An earlier shower had left the Island Highway damp, but the traffic was light and he quickly reached the Helmcken Road turnoff, which led to the Victoria General Hospital.

Directed to a nurses' station on the second floor of the plain, modern building, Greg identified himself and asked to see his dad. The desk nurse, an attractive but harried-looking young woman, eyed his solemn business suit, then reiterated his mother's warning. "He's probably asleep, Mr. Lothian." Was he mistaken, or was there a hint of relief in her voice? "But I guess you could look in for just a minute."

She pointed to a room at the end of the corridor. Walking as quietly as his stiff shoes would allow, Greg went down the hall and stopped in the doorway. The solitary bed in the room contained an old man, gaunt and pale, with a high forehead and a cascade of gray hair, lying very still. An IV line snaked down to one sinewy arm. The other lay across his chest, which rose and fell rhythmically.

A moment later, Walter Lothian's eyes snapped open. Evidently he recognized his son right away; the particular nuance of impatience in those dark, angry eyes was all too familiar. "Greg." The thin lips mouthed, though making no sound.

Greg edged into the room, eyes fixed upon his father. Up close, he could see that pain and irritation were muscling their way through a considerable degree of sedation. Anyone else would probably have been unconscious, but not this old warrior. "Hello, Dad," Greg said. "Sorry about what happened. How are you feeling?"

Walter Lothian's eyes flicked toward the ceiling, eloquently expressing his opinion of that banality. His free arm indicated a water glass on the bedside table, a gesture both feeble and commanding. Greg lifted the container and held it out. For all his care, a few drops spilled on the white stubble of his father's jaw, causing the reaching lips to take time out for a muttered imprecation. For the millionth time, Greg wondered how someone whose life's work involved the creation of beauty could be such a full-time curmudgeon. But he apologized as usual, better positioning the glass, and Walter drank. That done, he beckoned his son nearer. Hesitantly, Greg leaned in. "What is it, Dad?"

Walter took a slow, noisy breath. When words arrived, they were like a whisper from another room, but icily clear. "Your mother . . ."

"Mum? Yes, Dad, she's very worried about you."

"Shut up! Listen!"

"What . . . ?"

"It's not me she's worried about. The stupid idiot is scared for herself—about what I'll have to say—when I get out of here."

Greg could only stare. Despite the sedation, his father's pallid complexion was growing flushed. A heart monitor, unnoticed till now, began a strident bleat. "Dad!" Greg said in consternation, reaching out a hand and not knowing where to put it. "What are you talking about?"

"Foolish woman!" the old man spat, his voice growing in volume and intensity. "Senile, crazy old bitch! She's just lucky I *did* break my hip. Otherwise I might have wrung her neck."

Greg stepped back in dismay. There was a flurry at the door and a nurse appeared. She took in the yipping monitor and the patient's wrathful expression, then swung on Greg. "What's going on?" she snapped. "What have you been doing?"

"Nothing at all!" Greg stammered.

The nurse bustled across to the old man's bed. "I told you to look in on your father, Mr. Lothian," she said over her shoulder, "not get him all riled up. Don't you know he's got an operation in the morning?"

Speechless with fury, Greg said nothing. Having dismissed him, the nurse was fussing around the patient, muttering a small litany of soothing admonitions.

At this point, all Greg wanted was to be gone. He retreated to the door, but paused and looked back. His father seemed to have calmed somewhat, but his furious gaze was still fixed upon Greg, making him feel confused, irrationally ashamed and about nine years old.

"Damn you, old man," he muttered, and stalked out of the hospital.

TWO

Greg's first client arrived at ten the next morning, though he had been in the office since eight, working on what seemed liked a never-diminishing pile of returns. The routine of interspersing interviews with preparatory work was a distracting nuisance this late in the month, since 90 per cent of the discussions were unnecessary. It was almost a rule of thumb that the later clients left their meetings, the more they wanted to chat, a fact of life that Greg normally took in stride. But by the afternoon of this particular April 29, when he eventually forced himself to take a break, he was feeling more than ordinarily frazzled.

The underlying reason wasn't hard to understand. Last night's hospital visit had left a sour taste, filling his sleep with a jumble of unsettling dreams. He'd woken feeling irritable and depressed, a state which, despite the hectic nature of his day, remained in the background like a dull toothache. Since there was no question of taking time out for lunch, he'd picked up a sandwich on his way in to work. The phone rang, but he ignored it. There was no room for more appointments, which the girl at the front desk knew perfectly well. Any other business could just go into his voice mail. The ringing stopped, but almost immediately resumed. He began to get annoyed; reception must understand he was too busy for calls. He lifted the phone to tell them so, but got a surprise: there was the sound of sobbing on the line and then his mother's voice said, "Is that you, Greg?"

Guiltily, he realized that despite being angered by the visit to his father, he'd given little thought to what the old man was going through today. His mother's crying might have alerted him that something was amiss, but last night she'd also wept, about something quite silly, so his first reaction was impatience. "Yes, Mum, it's me. Calm down. Are you at the hospital?"

"Y—yes . . ."

"How did it go? How's Dad?"

"Greggie . . ." The childish diminutive, which only she used, came out like a half-strangled squeak, followed by a gulp and then dead air.

"Yes, Mum? What?"

"Greggie—Daddy's dead."

He heard the words clearly enough, but for a numb instant they had no meaning. When comprehension dawned, his first thought was that this was a prank, payback for his earlier lack of attention. At last, reason took hold, demolishing that sad evasion. "Dead?" he breathed. "I don't understand. I mean—*how*?"

The reply was a renewed sobbing. Another voice came on the line. "Mr. Lothian? Hello. This is Dr. York. I'm very sorry, sir, but I have to tell you that while under anesthetic, your father's heart just stopped. All the proper measures were taken, of course, but he could not be revived. There were no prior indications this might occur, but, sadly, such things do sometimes happen with the elderly. I'm so very sorry."

"Thank you."

"However, it's your mother I'm concerned about right now. She's naturally very distressed and all alone." The tone grew flat. "And she seems convinced that you are too busy to come to the hospital."

Greg felt his face flush. "What? Goodness, no. That's not the case at all."

"I'm glad. Then would you please come as soon as possible? Your mother needs you."

"Yes, yes. On my way," Greg said, but the connection was already broken. He put the phone down and stared at his desk in a stupor. The computer and the stack of files, the focus of his life until moments ago, seemed alien, yet they still possessed power, taunting him about the relentlessly looming deadline.

"Damn you, Dad!" The words slipped out, low and bitter, followed by the thought, *If you had to die, why did it have to be now?* Then, appalled at himself, he hurried out of the office.

The journey to the Victoria General took nearly twice as long as the previous night. In early afternoon, the expressway leading out of town was already clogged, and it was forty minutes before he reached the Helmcken turnoff. Finding a parking space took more time. When he finally entered the hospital, it was nearly an hour after his mother's call.

The waiting area to which Greg was directed at first appeared empty. Then he saw a figure in a far corner, slumped over and seeming pathetically small. Only when he arrived did she look up. At sixty-five, Mary Lothian was still an attractive woman, but now her body looked wasted, her face a sunken mask of grief. Her eyes were dark holes above sodden cheeks, and as soon as they lit on her son, they overflowed again. "Oh, Greggie," she whispered, "Daddy's gone. And it's all my fault."

That old refrain: if there were any fault, it lay with the lifelong ill temper that had, by all accounts, got his father into this mess. Crouching beside his mother, Greg put his arms around her, hugging her tightly. She clutched him with almost embarrassing abandon, which also made him feel unexpectedly tender. They remained entwined until his mother said at last, "Oh, dear. We must call Jill."

Greg's sister lived with her husband in Vancouver. Unlike Greg, she'd inherited a modicum of artistic talent, but had turned this toward practical ends. Starting in the graphics department of an advertising agency, she'd grown into a very successful account executive. Though she'd never got along with their father either, she had a similarly abrupt temperament. And it was with the old Walter Lothian "Don't mess with me" tone that she answered her phone now. "Jill Conroy."

"Hi, Jill. Me again."

"Greg! Why on Earth . . . ?" She broke off: evidently, her mind had been a long way away from the drama on Vancouver Island. "Oh—yes—right. How is Dad?"

He told her.

After it was done, he realized that his sister sounded less shocked than he'd anticipated, though he couldn't tell over the phone. He'd gone to the far end of the waiting room, where he could keep an eye on his mother while getting the worst part of the call over with. Now he started to walk back. "We're still at the hospital," he concluded. "Will you to talk to Mum?"

"No!" Jill said hurriedly. "I've a client here, and I can't handle it now. Tell Mum I'm sorry about Dad and I'll call her at home tonight. You'll be taking her back there, right?"

That gave Greg the opening he needed. "Jill, we have to talk about that. It's the end of April. You know what that means?"

Jill's voice was flat. "What?"

"For Christ's sake!" he said too loudly. His mother looked startled and he gave her a reassuring wave, moving farther away again. "Jill, listen—it's tax time. Till midnight tomorrow, I'm absolutely snowed. I'm sorry, but I shouldn't even be out of the office now. You've got to come over and help me here."

After only the slightest pause, his sister said, "Sorry, Greg. Not today."

"What! Please, listen . . ."

"No, *you* listen!" Jill said, with a clipped emphasis so biting that Greg winced. "I'm just as busy as you and my job's just as important. I don't care if it *is* 'tax time.' You're the one who's there, so you'll just have to cope. Tell Mum how sorry I am—and that I'll call her tonight. Bye."

His cell went dead. He shoved it away and returned to his mother. In the interim, someone had brought her tea, which she held as if it were a foreign object.

Greg passed along his sister's message, while his mind churned. With almost physical awareness, he could feel the seconds ticking toward tomorrow's midnight deadline. How many returns did he have to file before then? Too many, that was all he knew. "Mum . . ." he began.

Mary Lothian put down the tea mug with a clatter and rose to her feet. She looked tottery and frail, but her eyes held moist determination. "I want to see him," she said.

"Who?"

"Daddy. Before we leave, I must see him."

"But," Greg began, then gave up. His mother might be a passive soul, but there was a certain look she occasionally got that meant argument was useless. He went on a hunt, eventually finding someone to deal with his mother's wishes. He and Mary were ushered into a small room, tucked discreetly at the end of a side corridor. In it was a lone gurney bearing a sheet-shrouded figure. The accompanying nurse silently drew back the cover to reveal the face of the deceased.

In death, Walter Lothian had a remarkable expression; he actually looked benign, as serene as the paintings for which he was renowned. Greg was astonished, recalling all too vividly the anger that was his last memory of the living face. The contrast now was uncanny; it was like looking at a different person. His mother didn't seem so surprised; perhaps, Greg thought, she'd known some private, gentler Walter. That would explain why she'd put up with so much from him over the years. Or maybe he'd once been like this tranquil fellow on the gurney, and she was the only one who remembered. But no, he decided, the difference was likely just the result of gravity. Even the most restless spirits got smoothed out by a visit from the Grim Reaper: not so much relaxed as—gone.

Mary gave her son another surprise: in contrast to her earlier tears, she was quite calm. She stood for a time, silent and still, gazing dry-eyed at her husband's earthly remains. Finally she leaned down and kissed him tenderly. "I'm so sorry, darling," she murmured. "Please, forgive me."

Greg sighed inwardly. If his mother was still stubbornly determined to believe herself responsible for his dad's death, he supposed she was only running true to form. But it was certainly best not to dignify the fiction by appearing to pay too much attention. So he said nothing, standing quietly with his hand on her arm and waiting. His only thought was regret: in all the times he could recall being with his dad, this was the only one that remotely resembled peace.

THREE

Greg informed his office of the situation at the hospital, but told them not to be concerned. After taking his mother home, and finding someone to look after her, he'd be returning immediately. His intention then was to stay as long as it took, into the small hours, if necessary.

The only thing that the plan didn't take into account was his parents' old minivan. It was sitting out in the hospital lot and his mother insisted she couldn't leave it behind. Since chauffeuring her home in the van would make a swift return to town impossible, there was no alternative but to follow in his car. It was getting on to rush hour, so the trip on the winding Malahat Drive was painfully slow, all the more so because the new widow crawled like a zombie.

The fifty-kilometre drive north to Duncan took an hour, with another twenty minutes to reach the spot, upstream on the Cowichan River, where the family had a small acreage. The entrance to the property was off a rural byway, the driveway curving though a stand of fir and cedar to an open area beside the water. There the Lothian house stood, fully exposed on the river side, but backed by the dense woods, out of which it appeared to have thrust its way.

The vehicles arrived in time to intercept a figure coming around the building, from the direction of Walter's studio. It was a woman, dark-haired and petite, probably in her late twenties, with round, open features that to Greg were vaguely familiar. She glanced at him as he got out of his car, but her main focus was on his mother in the minivan.

Since Mary didn't move immediately, the woman went to the driver's door and opened it. The two stared at each other wordlessly. Communication must have passed, however, because the woman whispered, "Oh, God! Really?"

Stony-faced, Mary nodded.

"Oh, Mary, I'm very, very sorry!" the other replied. Then his mother tumbled from the car, and they were holding each other hard.

The newcomer turned out to be Lucy Lynley, whom Greg had known all his life but not set eyes on for years. Her parents had bought the adjoining property, downriver, and Lucy had been born there. As the only close neighbour, she had hung about the Lothian place, tagging along after Jill, who—three years older—had tartly tolerated her. Older still, Greg had had less contact with the irrepressible little girl. He remembered her for not being afraid of his dad—who, in turn, was far more tolerant of Lucy than of his own offspring. But at thirteen, she had been sent to school in Vancouver, and though she'd come home for holidays, Greg had rarely seen her after that. Now here she was, to him a near-stranger, though this was clearly not the case with his mother.

After a long time, the women disentangled. With hardly a glance in Greg's direction, they headed into the house. Feeling a trifle left out, he followed. Not till they were in the kitchen and, unbidden, Lucy was putting on the kettle, did his mother make introductions. "Oh, Greg, dear—Lucy," she said briefly. "Do you two remember each other?"

They both acknowledged that they did. Lucy, apparently very much at home in the house, smiled warmly. "I'm awfully sorry about your dad, Greg. It's a terrible shock. I'm going to miss him very much."

Greg was astonished. He remembered Lucy as an unusually candid person—which somehow endeared her to Walter, who'd squelched any such tendencies in his own family—so he had to believe her sincere. But missing his father? That idea was novel, to say the least.

As if reading his thoughts, his mother said, "Lucy moved back home when her own dad died, Greg. She's become a wonderful friend."

"Really?" Greg said, realizing that surprise had blinded him to the solution of a major problem. "Lucy, it's wonderful to meet you again, and I'm very glad you're here. Listen. could you—er—*stay* with my mum for a while?"

Lucy glanced at Mary, who shrugged. "Greg's just itching to get back to work."

Greg felt himself reddening. "It's not that I *want* to," he said hastily. "But I'm an accountant, and it's the end of April. Income tax time, you know. There's an absolutely huge pile of returns that have to be filed before midnight tomorrow."

"I understand," Lucy replied. "Your mum already told me about you."

"Great. So do you think you could do that—keep her company?"

Lucy's initial response shocked him: she laughed, then put her arms about his mother. "Greg, what do you think? Of course I will. I was going to offer anyway."

The whistling of the kettle drew her back to the stove, covering the moment of embarrassment. Greg's mother took his hand. Though her eyes shone with moisture, her face was composed. "Thank you for everything, dear," she said quietly. "I know how hard it's been—especially since you and poor Daddy didn't always see eye-to-eye—but you've been wonderful. I'll be all right. Lucy will be with me."

"Good." Relief let his mind begin to resume its usual preoccupations, reminding him of the other unfinished business. "Mum—er—it seems you forgot to send me the tax stuff. Want me to pick it up while I'm here?"

His mother looked surprised. "Tax stuff?"

"You know, your receipts and . . ."

"I know what you *mean*, dear. But I'm sure I sent it. I mailed it at least a couple of weeks ago."

"That's funny. Oh, well—don't worry. When it arrives, I'll get on to it. Bye, Mum. Call you later."

"Thank you. Off you go now."

Greg hugged his mother. She clung hard but briefly. Then, with a last peck on her cheek, and more awkward thanks to Lucy, he left the house, heading for his waiting tax returns.

FOUR

As it turned out, Greg met the tax-filing deadline without further incident. On the night of his father's death, he returned to the office and did indeed stay till the small hours. But after that he was well caught up, so on the following day, April 30, several hours before midnight, every last return was completed, checked, filed and sent zipping over the Internet to the domain of Revenue Canada.

It was only then that the full impact of what had transpired hit him. On his way home from the office in the early evening, stopped at the light at the intersection of Oak Bay Avenue and Foul Bay Road, he realized that he was feeling almost weepy. Surprise at the unexpected emotion was mingled with a sudden guilty concern; since he had left his mother yesterday, work had consumed him so completely that he had not even called her, as promised. Though phoning while driving was against his principles, he pulled out his cell anyway. After a couple of rings, a voice said, "Hello?" Not his mother, but a voice that it took him a moment to remember must be Lucy Lynley's.

"Oh, hey, Lucy," he blurted. "You're still there?"

Lucy gave her disconcertingly frank laugh. "Of course, Greg. What did you expect? I said I'd look after your mum."

He remembered that. Also that yesterday, frantic to get back to work, he'd more or less dumped his mother on their neighbour. Embarrassed, he muttered, "Right, yes, I'm sorry. How is she doing?"

"What can I say? As well as can be expected. She's napping right now. How's your tax thing going?"

"All finished—thanks to you."

She laughed again. "Thanks to your own hard work, I'm sure. When will you be here?"

Greg realized that it wasn't just exhaustion that had left his mind in such a jumble. He must be suffering from delayed shock, since he'd not even begun to think of what he had to do. "Actually, I'm headed out of town now," he lied. "If the traffic on the Malahat isn't too bad, I should be there in an hour."

"Okay. But drive safely. Your mother needs you in one piece, and I'm not going anywhere."

"Thanks, Lucy, You're very kind."

"Nonsense. I'm just doing what anyone would. See you when you get here."

"Yes. Goodbye!" Then, with a gesture that gave him uncharacteristic satisfaction, he made a U-turn right in the middle of sedate Oak Bay Avenue.

He arrived as the last reflections of sunset were fading on the Cowichan River. Briefly he sat, staring at the house, a fresh layer of reality surfacing as he realized that his mother would now be living here alone.

The place had started as a log cabin, one of the first homes on this section of Riverbottom Road, built before the Second World War. Later owners had added a frame addition on one side, and cleared the land to give a better view of the river. Walter Lothian had acquired the property in the 1970s, when his paintings were beginning to gain national attention. Growing prosperity had allowed him to add yet another wing, a post-and-beam structure with a more-than-passing resemblance to a Coast Salish longhouse, plus a substantial studio, connected to the main building by a breezeway. The resulting agglomeration had mellowed with time and weather into a pleasantly harmonious whole, a fitting abode—as noted in arts supplements—for an important Canadian painter. In his youth, Greg had disliked the place, with its artsy clutter, and hated the isolation. Only later, after he'd created his own orderly space in Victoria, did he occasionally miss it, though nothing would have induced him to live there again.

Now, in the dying day, it looked, paradoxically, both brooding and cozy. Light glowed through the living room windows and in the front hall. Greg got out of the car, crossed the broad front deck and entered quietly. His mother must have awakened, for her voice could be heard from the kitchen. Greg headed in that direction, then paused. Though he couldn't make out what was being said, something about the tone made him apprehensive—and feel almost as if he were eavesdropping. He retreated to the front door and slammed it, calling loudly, "Hello! I'm back." Only then did he walk into the kitchen.

His mother and Lucy were sitting at the table, a pot of tea between them. Both women looked around as Greg appeared, and he stopped short, caught by their expressions. Mary looked stricken, her face matching the tone that he'd heard from the hallway. What stunned him was Lucy. Gone was the sedate young woman he'd met yesterday and later talked with. The person who confronted him now was pale with shock and some deep emotion.

Greg had only a moment to register this, for Lucy composed herself and rose swiftly.

Forcing her features into the caricature of a smile, she came to him, impulsively taking his hand. The contact was brittle with tension. "Oh, good, you're here at last," she said quickly. "Your mother will be so relieved."

"Yes. But what . . . ?"

"Now I must be off," Lucy continued, without pause. "Mary, I'm so sorry about everything. But Greg's here now. If there's anything more I can do, please let me know. Goodbye. I'll see myself out."

Lucy let go of Greg's hand, using it to literally launch herself in the direction of the hall. A moment later came the sound of the front door closing.

Her departure was so instantaneous that Greg was at a loss for words. What had caused Lucy's manner to change so dramatically? It had to be whatever Mary had been saying when he arrived. But what could be so dreadful as to cause that reaction? Instinct told him that he didn't want to know. And when he turned back, he was relieved, albeit freshly surprised, to see his mother calmly pouring more tea.

"Did you get your work finished, dear?" she asked quietly.

"Yes, Mum, thanks. Sorry I had to run off yesterday." He wanted to ask how she was feeling, but that seemed crass and obvious, so he continued lamely, "But I'm here now. And Jill will be over on the weekend, to—you know—help with the arrangements and everything."

"I understand," Mary said. "You're both good children. Daddy knew that, you know, though he didn't always show it. Lucy's a nice girl too. So open and honest. Hasn't changed a bit since she was a child."

She sure changed a lot in the last hour, Greg thought. But he said, "It certainly was a surprise to see her again yesterday."

"She's been coming around a lot since she moved back. We've become real friends. Did you know that Daddy was giving her lessons?"

The revelations were coming thick and fast. "Lessons?"

"Painting lessons. She's very good, as a matter of fact." Mary put down her teacup. "Want to see?"

Bemused, he stared, unable to read her. Something was going on here, more than just reaction to the recent tragedy, but he couldn't make it out. Masking it—or maybe part of it—was this strange charade. "See what?"

"Lucy's work. Come on!"

On the back of the kitchen door hung a familiar, old blue sweater. Mary heaved it on and took Greg's arm, leading him out and along the deck to the breezeway to his father's studio. This was a large building, finished in cedar board and batten, with windows on the river side and several skylights positioned for north light. The entrance was a heavy door, painted with Coast Salish designs, which swung inward to reveal the full sweep of the studio.

It was a veritable forest of paintings; every wall was hung with them, as high as the rafters, and easels displayed several more, in various stages of completion. In many places, except against the big wood stove in the centre of the room, canvasses were stacked six and eight deep. The subject of this vast outpouring of creativity was the wilderness of Vancouver Island: landscapes and seascapes, birds and animals and fish, in infinite variety and exquisite detail; form and composition, light and colour, drama and design, all treated with vibrant energy and consummate skill. Greg, who'd known this place since childhood, his familiarity blending with an innate—or perhaps reactionary—indifference, drew a sharp breath. Was it the length of time he'd been absent? Had more art appreciation seeped into his unwilling soul than he'd realized? Or was it simply that the turbulent creator of all this had finally departed? Whatever the reason, for the first time in his life, his father's work truly moved him. "Wow!" he breathed.

After putting on the lights, his mother had paused at the door. "You sound surprised."

"I guess I am."

"You'd forgotten how wonderful his work is?"

"I don't think I ever realized."

She took hold of his arm again, surveying the studio fervently. "He was a master, Greggie. BC's very best. If he'd only known how to market himself, like some of those others, we might have been rich. Then perhaps, it wouldn't have mattered . . ."

Greg felt a prickling at the back of his neck. "Mattered? What?"

Instead of answering, his mother led him to the far end of the studio, stopping in front of a small easel with a modest-sized canvas.

This painting was different from the rest: a landscape, less dramatic in form and not so spectacularly deft, but with a shimmering, airy quality that was quite magical. "This is what I wanted to show you," his mother said.

"Lucy's work?"

"What do you think?"

"I'm impressed."

"Daddy thought she was very talented, and I never heard him say that about anyone. He was going to . . ." She broke off, gazing at the painting. Her grip shifted to his hand, which she held in a tight grip. "Greggie?"

"Mum?"

"If it were up to you—would you let Lucy keep using the studio?"

He felt the neck-prickling again. "What do you mean, 'up to me'? That's for you to say."

"Of course. Never mind." She leaned up and kissed him, administering a quick, fierce hug. "You're a good son, Greggie. I'm sorry Daddy was always so busy. That he wasn't—nicer to you. Now, because of—what happened—he'll never get a chance to . . ."

The words drifted into silence. Greg waited, but a conclusion never came. From Lucy's painting, his mother's eyes moved outward, scanning the whole studio. Afterwards, she took a deep breath and stepped back. "Thank you, dear."

"What for?"

"Being here. Being you. Now, you really should get some rest. I know that's what I'm going to do. Good night." She slipped out the door, a wraith drifting into the dark.

Greg stood for a long time, contemplating his father's handiwork: shining beauty created by a man who had rarely spoken a civil word. Then he roused himself and went back into the house. The place felt peaceful at last, the sadness muted, the strange tableau that had confronted him on his arrival now almost like a dream. Whatever it had been about, he was too exhausted to care.

At the end of a corridor leading off the kitchen, Greg could see light under his mother's door, and he decided to wait until it went out before going to bed. Wandering aimlessly, he remembered where his father's whisky stash had always been kept. He checked and, sure enough, in a cupboard over the sink were some bottles of Glenfiddich. Single-malt Scotch was not usually his drink, but now it seemed like a very good idea. He found a glass, poured a shot and downed it. The strong liquor burned, but then he was rewarded with a pleasant buzz, the best feeling he'd had for a long time. He poured another shot, drinking it more slowly as he moved out of the kitchen, circling through the rest of the house, idly examining familiar objects, the whisky doing its slow, blessed work until the glass was empty and he was back in the kitchen again.

By then half an hour had passed, and he saw that the light under his mother's door was still on. Either she couldn't sleep or she'd passed out. Suspecting the latter, he decided to slip in and kill the light, so it wouldn't wake her prematurely. Only when he reached the bedroom door did he realize that it was ajar. Slowly he pushed it open, to discover the room flooded with light, the big bed unmade and quite empty.

As was the room itself.

On the far side, French doors led onto a patio, overlooking a broad stretch of lawn that ran down to the river. One of these was open, drapes billowing fitfully in the night breeze.

Greg stood quite still, while his heart, which the whisky had soothed, began to pick up speed again. He started to call out, then stopped, knowing this to be useless. Instead, he strode across the room, thrust aside the curtains and peered out. The patio was also deserted. Light from the house streaked across the lawn, a slash of yellow reaching almost to the river.

Without thought or decision, he was racing, across the patio and the lawn, his shadow preceding him like a monster down the slick corridor of light. At the end of this, beside the softly whispering water, he found it: a small pile of clothing, neatly folded—and on the top, his mother's old blue sweater.

FIVE

Greg drove north on the Trans-Canada Highway, turning off near the small town of Ladysmith onto Cedar Road. His destination was five kilometres along this road and was impossible to miss, so he'd been told. He drove for a long time amidst semi-woodland and scattered farms, and just as he was thinking that he had indeed missed it—there it was: lawns and flowers and a forest of tiny memorial plaques, neat and cheery in the spring sunshine. Beyond, a looming presence, masked by a funeral chapel and with, happily, no smoke rising from its stubby stack, was the crematorium.

Off to one side of the complex was the general office. The sun was hot on Greg's back as he trudged across the parking lot, adding physical discomfort to his gloom. It would have been a relief to remove his suit jacket but, considering his errand, that might have seemed frivolous. So it was with relief that he entered the office, though the hardest part of this dismal exercise was yet to come.

"Good afternoon," he said to the attendant, trying to make his voice as natural as possible. "My name is Gregory Lothian. I've come to pick up my parents' remains."

The attendant was a pale young man whose sombre suit seemed a size too big. "Yes, of course, Mr. Lothian," he replied, in surprisingly well-modulated tones. "Mother or father?"

This was it, the question he had been dreading. He took a deep breath. "Er—both, actually."

It was spoken, the clue that would probably alert the attendant to the uncomfortable situation. How many double cremations could they have, after all? And they'd hardly be unaware of the unfortunate publicity these particular deaths had engendered: the naked body of the wife of a well-known artist dragged from the Cowichan River three days after his own unexpected demise. Mortifying, to say the least.

In the news reports, the word suicide had never been mentioned, but what sixty-five-year-old woman went innocently skinny-dipping in April, right after her husband's death? So the facts were pretty obvious. As if this weren't bad enough, the body had been discovered by some native fishermen on a snag below the Native Heritage Centre, hung up for all the world to gawk at. Since it lacked ID and was battered about by the current, foul play had been suspected. Though the truth had swiftly emerged, this added a falsely sensational undertone to a sad tale which, due to the Lothian reputation, had already received too much press coverage. It had had a few days to die down, but Greg still felt cold embarrassment as he identified the subjects of his sad errand.

"Mr. and Mrs. Lothian, yes," the attendant said, with neutral solemnity. Was that a knowing flicker in his eyes as he produced the file? Greg wasn't sure, but at least nothing was said, which was a relief. Forms were provided for signature and discreet information offered about the availability of a variety of services. Greg declined everything but the ashes.

Grim task over, nervousness replaced by relief, Greg retraced his steps across the parking lot, now the possessor of two plain carrier bags, each with a plastic cylinder containing what was left of one of his parents.

He got into his car, depositing the bags on the floor in front of the passenger seat. Then, feeling this to be somehow inappropriate, he shifted the bags to the seat itself. He'd done little more than glance inside, since the contents gave him a sick feeling, but his overwhelming reaction was still mostly amazement. A week ago, the individuals represented by these anonymous containers had been vibrantly alive. Then, apparently, something appalling had happened. Causing a rage in Walter, it had precipitated the events that had run their brief but fatal course. What this dread "something" was, Greg still had no idea. He just knew that his mother had considered herself somehow responsible. And his father had evidently passionately agreed. The old man's words at their last fateful meeting still rang in his mind: "She's just lucky I *did* break my hip. Otherwise I might have wrung her neck." Sickeningly extreme, even for Walter. But the cause of all this was still a mystery.

Greg turned on the ignition and prepared to depart. He put on his seatbelt, dismissing a ridiculous impulse to do the same for his companions. The car's electric motor made no sound as he slipped out of the bright gardens and headed home.

Apart from brief notices in the Victoria *Times Colonist* and the Duncan papers, Greg had as yet done nothing about memorial arrangements. His father had been a devout atheist and his mother, typically, never dared to express any conflicting views, so he had no guidelines. When he had contacted his sister with news of the second tragedy, she'd been shocked and, he felt sure, genuinely grieved, especially by the manner of their mother's death. But she'd seen no need for a formal ceremony. Remarking that he surely didn't want her to come and hold his hand, she'd made it clear she wasn't coming to the island anytime soon. But she hadn't been embarrassed to ask one question: had he seen anything of a will? He hadn't, but said he'd look and let her know when he'd found it, and they'd left it at that. If nothing else, that conversation made one thing clear: however untimely the older Lothians' deaths, there hadn't been a real family for a long time.

Twenty-five minutes after leaving the crematorium, Greg found himself on the strip of auto dealerships and fast-food outlets that skirt the city of Duncan. He'd been heading for Victoria, then realized that he didn't want to have the ashes in his apartment. The idea of them sitting on his coffee table, or even tucked away in some cupboard, was too unsettling right now. So in Duncan, he turned right at the Trunk Road light and headed west.

In fact, there was one thing that held a clue to whatever had occasioned his parents' deaths. Greg had left town, passed the hospital on Gibbins Road, and was almost at the Riverbottom turnoff when he recalled it: the extraordinary change he had observed that last night in Lucy Lynley. Meeting her the first time, then talking later on the phone, he had thought the young woman seemed confident and very secure, just as he'd remembered her. But at their final encounter, she had been disturbed—the word that came to mind was "aghast"—and this was almost certainly because of something told her by Mary.

The entrance to the Lothian property was a regular farm gate, fronting the gravel driveway that wound through the trees toward the river. Greg opened the gate and drove slowly down, stopping in front of the deserted house. In the days immediately following his mother's death, there had been considerable activity here, mainly by police, at first searching, and then, after the body was found, reiterating explanations and clearing up details for the coroner. That concluded, Greg had closed up and escaped. Home in Victoria, he fitfully immersed himself in work while trying to adjust to the tragedy. That brief hiatus was ended by the call from the crematorium.

Now he was back at the house. Specifically, his purpose had been to store the ashes. But as soon as he emerged from the car—stretching his back while taking in the silent and already forlorn-looking scene of his childhood—he knew it was going to be more than that.

It was Saturday, so he didn't have to be back in town for a day and a half. This would be an ideal time to get started on what he'd so far avoided thinking about: the depressing business of sorting out his parents' affairs.

He entered the house, noting its musty and deserted feeling. His footsteps echoed as he moved from room to room, and although the day was still bright, he found himself putting on lights. When he got to the door of the master bedroom, he paused, vividly recalling the moment when he'd stood there, thinking that his mother was sleeping. Then, when he'd entered, he'd found emptiness, the gaping French door, blowing curtains—harbingers of the great sea-change about to be visited on his life. And on the bed, the only sign of a mother he would not see again until days later on a mortuary slab: the head-dent in a solitary pillow.

To Greg's mild alarm, that depression was still there. Putting down the bags containing the ashes, he hurried to the bed, smoothed the quilt and plumped the pillow, removing all disquieting traces of its last occupant, then straightened and looked enquiringly about. In the far corner was a big old English wardrobe, a necessity, for this room had no built-in closet. That would suit his purpose well enough. As he went to open the wardrobe, his image in the door-mirror stared back, a tense, pale young man, in a business suit that looked a trifle pompous. Greg grimaced at the image and opened the door. The clothes hanging there were mainly his mother's, but the odour was not: pipe tobacco and linseed oil and paint, the all-pervading smell of the artist's studio. *God, you old bugger!* Greg thought. *Even here, in Mum's own wardrobe, you still managed to dominate her.*

But at the back, behind the clothes, was what he needed: a place to store—he would not let himself think of it as hide—the ashes. Thrusting aside the garments, he tucked the bags, side by side, in the dark. "There!" he muttered. "Now you two will just have to work things out."

Hearing himself, feeling foolish and weirdly giggly, he closed the door and hurried back through the house.

SIX

After dealing with the ashes, Greg realized that he badly needed to get out of his suit. It was his everyday apparel in town, but it seemed, in the present surroundings, not only uncomfortable but faintly ridiculous. His old room at the far end of the house had been turned into a sort of office—by his mother, no doubt, since Walter had never soiled his fingers with practicalities—but the bed was still there. Also remaining was a well-remembered chest of drawers, containing some of the clothes he kept here for his rare visits. He rooted out some jeans and a sweater, exchanging these for his more formal attire, which he draped neatly on the bed.

Only then did he pay proper attention to the room itself. The most obvious change since his own time was the addition of a battered but substantial rolltop desk. Feeling like an intruder, Greg reached for the catch and found it unlocked. The top emitted a throaty rattle as it rolled up. What was revealed looked to his orderly eye like disaster: papers and letters and bills and chequebooks and bric-a-brac obscured the desktop completely. In the centre of the pile, balanced like a climber on an alpine summit, was a shallow basket, and in this, neatly folded and tied with a ribbon, was a document. Greg picked it up and read the inscription: *Last Will and Testament of Walter Lothian*

Well, that was one problem solved. Obviously, the document had been purposely placed for easy discovery. Unexpected, however, were the words handwritten below the title:

Greg and Jill—I don't have one—but everything you need is in here—so you can share what is left. I love you, Mum.

And underneath, an almost savage scrawl:

DARLINGS—PLEASE FORGIVE ME—I'M SO SORRY FOR BEING SO STUPID.

As motionless as the cold house, Greg gazed at the will. Presently, with surprise, he realized that some of the handwritten part had become blurred. There was wetness on the paper—dripping from himself. It took the sudden and violent heaving of his shoulders to alert him to what was happening.

A while later, he came out of what felt like a trance to find himself at the kitchen table. A glass and a bottle of whisky were in front of him; his father's will was also there. He took another sip of the drink he'd poured. Now more familiar with the relief it provided, he realized with surprise that Glenfiddich might have been the one thing that kept his querulous parent sane. Then he untied the ribbon on the will and unfolded it.

A quick glance with his practised eye revealed it to be a very standard document, an anticlimax after the emotions its discovery had evoked. Following the usual statements, stipulations and disclaimers, it went on to leave everything to Walter's wife, and then, should she predecease him, equally to his children. Greg was named as executor, which he remembered long ago agreeing to do. That was it. If anything was noteworthy, it was how clear-cut and simple it was, and how fair. Knowing his old man, Greg wouldn't have been surprised to find himself disinherited, or the whole kit and caboodle willed to the Sierra Club.

Which made what had been scrawled on the outside of the will even stranger. *Forgive me.* Why? *So sorry for being so stupid.* About what, for God's sake?

Greg pushed aside the will and stood up from the table. Feeling woozy, he realized that he hadn't eaten since breakfast, a situation not helped by his unaccustomed indulgence in his father's tipple. The well-stocked kitchen had plenty of ingredients for a quickly thrown-together supper. He made a sandwich and heated a can of soup, which he consumed with some freshly brewed coffee. When he'd finished, he felt better, but the restored strength only added intensity to the renewed turmoil in his head.

Whatever his mother had done—that deed darkly hinted at even before his father's death, which had found its final expression in the cryptic scribblings on the will—it could be ignored no longer. Before he could think straight, he simply had to find out what had happened.

Fortunately, there was one place where he might be able to do that. Clearing the dishes and washing up gave him time to figure out a plan of action. Courage to go about it was provided by another shot of the old man's Scotch.

Ready at last, he went to the back door, where outdoor garments were traditionally hung. With reluctance, he selected an ancient leather jacket that had belonged to his father. It was stiff with age, and it reeked. He put it on anyway, finding it surprisingly comfortable. *If you could see me now,* he thought, trying without success to picture his father's expression.

He went out the door, around the studio and down toward the river. Giving a wide berth to the spot where he'd found the clothing, he moved downstream, coming at last to the path that led through the woods to the property next door: the home of Lucy Lynley.

SEVEN

The Lynley house was the polar opposite of the Lothian sprawl, a neat, improbably suburban bungalow, tucked snugly into a clearing. Here, the river took a turn to the south, so although the property had frontage on the water, the dwelling itself was some distance away. At this point in the river, the current was swift—a fact not lost on Greg, who still found it difficult not to picture what it had so recently borne away—and on the far side, the land rose rapidly, blocking what was left of the sun.

Lucy's father, Marv, Greg recalled, had worked in some capacity for the regional district. A small, wiry fellow who'd always seemed to be grinning, he was the first adult male who had not made Greg nervous. With a parent like that, it was not hard to see where Lucy had got her confidence. Now he too was dead, apparently. Like her daughter, Shirl Lynley had been forthright and pleasant, but Greg couldn't remember much else about her.

There were lights on in the house. As he approached, a motion-sensor lamp came on at the front. His shoes scrunched on gravel, eliciting a commotion of barking. A moment later a black shape hurtled into view from the rear of the house. Greg stepped hurriedly onto the porch, back turned to the door, but the dog was a young Lab intent only on licking him to death. While fending off the canine enthusiast, Greg heard the door open behind him.

"Oh, my God!" a voice cried.

Greg straightened and turned, to find Lucy staring at him in shock, which was replaced immediately by a surprised laugh. "Oh, it's *you*!" she said, in bemused tones.

"Who did you think it was?" Greg asked.

Lucy grabbed the still-leaping animal, holding his collar. "This guy's pretty well trained, really, but with new people he gets so excited he forgets everything he knows. Calm down, Hatch. Sit!" The dog obeyed. "Good boy!" Lucy said and then, to Greg, "Sorry about that."

"It's okay. But it seems like I gave you a shock."

"It's just that when I opened the door and saw that jacket, for a moment I thought—well, you know—that it was your dad."

"Oh." Greg glanced down in distaste. "Yeah, I guess that'd scare anyone." Then, realizing how callous that sounded under the circumstances, he went on hastily, "I hope I haven't come at a bad time."

"No, no." Lucy held the door for him to enter, keeping the dog out, and shut it firmly. "Greg, I'm so sorry about your mother. It's terrible. So utterly tragic and sad. I can't begin to tell you how bad I feel."

They stood in the hallway, awkward at first, saying the things that needed to be said. Over the last days, Greg had given little thought to Lucy, the revelation of her new relationship to his family having been pushed into the background. Guiltily, he realized that it was only because he wanted something that he'd come here at all. Yet once he started talking, he found that he was glad. As he spoke, not just relating events but also revealing his feelings, largely unacknowledged until now, it was as though his insides began to unwind. When he got to the part about discovering the will, he didn't even omit the detail of the unexpected tears, nor the solace he had found in his father's Scotch. He told it all, a lot more than he'd known there was to tell. When he was done, he felt surprisingly relieved.

Only then did he become aware of other sounds in the house: low voices and the canned laughter of a TV audience from somewhere nearby. Seeing him glance in that direction, Lucy said, "Goodness. Mum! Come on. I know she'll want to see you."

Greg followed Lucy to a living room at the far end of the hall. Like the house itself, this was quite formal, with plain, well-kept furniture and—Greg couldn't help noticing—one of his father's paintings. The fireplace crackled with a cozy blaze, beside which, in a deep recliner, sat Lucy's mother.

Although Greg recognized Shirl Lynley easily enough, he was astonished at the change in her. She could not, he felt sure, be much older than his mother had been, but she looked more like eighty, her face deeply lined, her hair pure white. However, her eyes were bright and alive, the clear model for her daughter's, and as Greg and Lucy entered, they lit up, transforming her sombre features.

"Hello, Greg," Shirl said, turning off the TV. "I'm sorry for your loss. It's lovely to see you again after so long—I'm just so sad it had to be like this." Only when she held out her hand did Greg notice the final detail of the scene: placed within easy reach were two stout walking sticks.

Listening to her kindly words, Greg felt grateful and unexpectedly moved. But one thing kept nagging at the back of his mind: the real purpose for his visit. As soon as he could, he made his excuses and bade Shirl good night. Lucy caught up with him in the hall. "Do you have to leave so soon?"

"Not really. But the reason I came by is to ask you an awkward question, and I didn't want to distress your mother. I'm sorry to see her looking so frail, by the way. Is she unwell?"

Lucy nodded sadly. "MS. It developed after my dad died. For a while the progress seemed quite slow, but not anymore. Unfortunately, she's a diabetic, too. That's the main reason why I came to live back home."

"I'm sorry to hear it."

"Yes, it's dreadful for her, but we do the best we can." Lucy led the way into a room at the other end of the house. "Okay, what's your question?"

The room had a window overlooking the garden. Greg went to it and stared out at a fast-fading sunset. "Lucy, I need to know what it was that my mother told you on that last night. When I arrived, you looked so shocked, and bolted out so abruptly, I knew it had to be something dreadful. And important. But she didn't tell me. And later—well—she walked into the river. Now I've become sort of obsessed about it."

After a pause, Lucy said, "I guess I'm not surprised."

"Then please tell me."

"All right." She moved in closer. "But first I must ask you one thing. Had your mother told you what was wrong with her?"

Greg frowned. "Wrong? What do you mean?"

"Damn!" Lucy muttered. "I told her she shouldn't keep it from you and Jill."

"What, for God's sake?"

"Greg, your mother had cancer."

Greg all but gasped. He had no idea what he'd expected, but that certainly wasn't it. After he'd had time to recover a little, Lucy told him the whole story. Several months earlier, Mary had been diagnosed with a form of leukemia, slow but eventually lethal. Chemotherapy was the accepted treatment, but it was a doubtful remedy, with side-effects arguably worse than the disease. Somehow she'd found out about a clinic in Mexico that offered more benign—and arguably as effective—natural remedies. With her husband's encouragement, she'd arranged to go there for treatment.

At this point Greg interrupted. "Natural remedies? What are we talking about here?"

"I'm not sure exactly. I remember her mentioning apricot pits, something called Laetrile. She didn't tell me too much about that part."

"You say my dad agreed to all this?"

"Evidently."

"Wow!"

"Why so surprised? You think he didn't care about your mum?"

"No. I've often thought she was the only person in the world he *did* care about, though that didn't stop him treating her like a slave. But alternative therapies? Mexico? It doesn't sound the kind of thing he'd go for."

Lucy shook her head decidedly. "That just shows how little you knew him. You're so straight yourself, so . . ."

"Anal?"

"I was going to say conservative. Anyway, the direct opposite of your parents. Being non-conformists—a couple of old hippies, basically—they were just the people to go for unconventional medicine. And although Walter pretended to be an old tyrant, he really was a softie underneath. From the time I was a kid, I knew that. Look at his painting. That should tell you."

Greg shook his head. "You're incredible."

"Why?"

"Either you're completely nuts or you knew my dad better than anyone."

Lucy shrugged. "Be that as it may. The point is, he did agree to the Mexico treatment, even though it was going to cost a small fortune. He told Mary to cash in some of the bonds they had to pay for it. They'd booked into the clinic—it's down in Baja California—and they were going to leave last week. But then . . ."

"My dad broke his hip, so they couldn't go?"

"Not exactly."

"What, then?"

"Your dad broke his hip *because* they couldn't go."

Greg felt dizzy. "Now I'm completely confused."

"I'm not surprised," Lucy sighed. "It's complicated—and dreadful—so I'd better start at the beginning. You probably know that Walter never approved of credit, right? Mary did the actual managing, but with him everything had to be either cash or cheque; he was old-fashioned like that. They did have a bank card at the end, but only because it was necessary and free. And that turned out to be their mistake."

"The bank card?"

"Indirectly. You see, the treatment in Mexico was going to cost twenty thousand dollars, and it had to be paid in advance. That in itself wasn't a problem. They'd sold their securities, and they had the money. The thing was how to get it to the clinic. Their debit card wouldn't work from Mexico, and they didn't want to be carrying all that cash. The solution was a cashier's cheque, and they had the funds all ready in their account to buy one."

"What happened?"

"A couple of days before Mary was due to get the cheque, she got a phone call. The caller identified himself as an account inspector."

Greg frowned. "Account inspector? What kind of nonsense is that?"

"Just that: nonsense. You're an accountant, so naturally you know that. But your parents had spent their lives avoiding the modern world. When the call came, your dad was working, but your mum was the one who always did the business anyway, so she took it. This 'inspector' was a con artist, of course, but very plausible and clever. He told a scary story about the bank's computer being broken into by hackers, and a whole lot of convincing garbage about needing to freeze accounts in order to stop them being plundered. To do this, he asked for their account numbers, passwords and codes and . . ."

"She *gave* them to him?"

"Everything!"

"Oh, Christ!"

"Thinking that she'd done the right thing, saving their precious Mexico fund, your mother was very relieved. At the time, she didn't even tell your dad, figuring he had enough on his mind. But a few days later, when she called at the bank to pick up her precious cashier's cheque, there was no money. The account had been cleaned out. Of course, your mum was devastated. But somehow she got herself home, and then she had no choice but to tell Walter."

"I'm amazed she dared."

"Apparently, she thought the only way was to bite the bullet and get it over with. That was her final mistake. She went out to the studio where he was working and just—told him. Your dad was first shocked, and then furious. He threw down his brush and took a blind run at her. I don't suppose he even knew what he was going to do. Whatever it was, he never got the chance. He tripped over an easel and fell down hard and . . . well, you know the rest."

Outside it was now night, the sky as dark as the mood that had descended on the little room. As the full import of what he'd been told filtered, layer by layer, into Greg's mind, he felt the last residue of the paralysis that had possessed him, ever since he had found his mother's clothes by the river, finally depart. Replacing it was a still, cold rage, making him feel not just released, but powerful, more strangely alive than he had felt in a long time. *Account inspector!* he thought savagely. *If I could lay my hands on him right now, I'd kill the bastard.* But none of this emotion showed on his face.

He said quietly, "I can see why you were so shocked. That story must have been terrible to hear, and even harder to tell. So, for what it's worth, thank you."

"I'm just sorry I had to be the messenger. Now that you know, does it help you to understand what happened?"

Greg shrugged. "I guess it has to. One other thing. On the night she died, my mum said something that—I realize now—should have been a clue as to what she intended. She asked if I'd let you keep using Dad's studio."

Lucy looked astonished. "Really?"

"At the time I didn't know what she meant. But now I can answer. My dad was a difficult guy, but it seems in some ways you knew him better—and certainly stood up to him more—than any of us. So, as far as I'm concerned, you should feel free to come and go, use the studio, or whatever, all you want."

"You're very kind."

Greg smiled, feeling—considering his still-simmering anger—absurdly gallant. "It's my pleasure. Now I must be getting along."

As he turned away, she stopped him with a gentle touch. "Are you going to be all right?"

"I've no idea. I'll know better when I've decided what I'm going to do about all this."

"What *can* you do?"

Greg shrugged. "Don't know that either. But you can be very sure—*something.*"

EIGHT

Cowichan, which in the Coast Salish tongue means "warm land," is the name borne by a number of geographic features on the south end of Vancouver Island. The Cowichan Valley is a fertile depression bounded in the west by the spine of the island and on the east by the ocean. Cowichan Lake is an extensive body of water sitting at the upper end of the valley. This, in turn, is drained by a river of the same name, which winds eastward for forty kilometres until, after skirting the city of Duncan, it empties into the sea at Cowichan Bay. In winter, this waterway can be a swift torrent, barely tamed by control gates at the lake end, saved from flooding only by the high, wooded banks that confine most of its length. For the rest of year, the flow is more benign—host to fishermen, swimmers and tube-riders galore—but even then, it is never less than lively, demanding care and respect.

Upon rising on the morning after he talked to Lucy, Greg's first action was to make coffee and walk down to the river. No longer did he try to avoid the place where his mother had launched herself into the hereafter; indeed, he went there purposely. Though his face showed no emotion, his mind hummed with a continuous background harmonic of anger, as strong and as cold as the waters flowing by.

Deliberately, he gazed at the spot where the sad pile of his mother's clothes had lain, letting the memory act as a spur to the resolve that was hardening within. What action this would produce he did not know, but the stimulus was necessary. All his life had been spent gently, in mild pursuits, top priority going always to the avoidance of conflict. This had brought comfort and security, but also isolation and loneliness, alienation from the people who had given him being. "You don't know what you've got till it's gone." The sentiment from the old song had an uncomfortably appropriate resonance right now. His family—all but his semi-stranger sister—was certainly gone, dispatched in little more than the blink of an eye. That he was not to blame didn't matter. That nothing would ever change what had happened was not the point. If life was not to be completely meaningless, eventually he had to make some kind of response.

With that understanding firmly in mind, Greg returned to the house, showered, made breakfast, then set about the obvious things that needed doing. He'd already decided to take some time off work; since he had vacation time accumulated and May was slack, this wouldn't be a problem. But because it was Sunday, he couldn't tell his employers till tomorrow. The rest of the day he spent tidying and sorting and exploring the "office." Though it had once been his bedroom, he wasn't sleeping there, using his sister's room instead.

As executor, it was his legal duty to sort out his parents' affairs, no small task, but one for which training and temperament made him well qualified. The rolltop desk where he'd discovered the will was the obvious starting point. The chaotic jumble of its contents no longer bothered him; creating order from other people's mess was, after all, what he did every day. By the end of the day, the first winnowing was done: bills, receipts, correspondence, bank statements were all organized into piles, ready to be gone through later in greater detail.

In the process, Greg came across a brochure for the cancer clinic, two round-trip tickets to Los Angeles, and a schedule—but no tickets—for an airline offering connector flights to Mexico. So there it was: physical evidence of a dream that had been shattered. The final piece of the sad puzzle he found not in the desk, but in a nearby corner, as if it had been flung there: an old-style bank passbook, with the deposits and withdrawals neatly itemized. The final entries told the tale all too clearly. A month ago, there had been a deposit for twenty thousand dollars, proceeds from the securities that had been sold. Then later, four withdrawals were itemized in rapid succession, five thousand dollars each, with the closing balance—the discovery of which had set off the fateful plunge to catastrophe—zero.

Greg took the passbook back to the kitchen. He got out the whisky and poured himself a shot, discovering with surprise that, since the night of the tragedy, he'd managed to go through most of a bottle. Well, who cared? His father wasn't going to need it anymore. During his lifetime, he'd done little enough to promote his son's peace of mind, so it was only fitting that he should provide some small comfort now, if only via the medium of his liquor supply. This, in fact, was substantial; Greg discovered half a case of Glenfiddich in the cupboard. The old man, at least in that regard, had evidently not felt the need to stint himself.

Greg downed the first shot and poured another. While he ate supper, he examined the pathetic little passbook again. By that time, he had pretty much decided on the next thing he needed to do.

Next morning, when he phoned his parents' bank in Duncan, he got an appointment for that afternoon. A hunt through the Yellow Pages then provided a local lawyer who could fit him in within a day: it had been in his mind to apply for probate of the will himself, but, uncharacteristically, he decided he wasn't in the mood to tackle the minor legal formalities. Even his customary business suit felt oddly uncomfortable when he donned it to go into town; living at his parents' place seemed to be having a strange effect on him.

The fifteen-minute drive into Duncan, winding by the river, then through the woods and across the brief stretch of farmland that merged into the outskirts of the town, was an experience so anciently familiar that he hardly noticed. By then his mind was already at the bank, running through the confrontation to come. Of one thing at least he was certain: those people were going to be made to feel very bad for their part in what had happened to his parents.

Downtown Duncan, however, did give him a surprise. It had changed from the sleepy village of his youth into quite a cool little metropolis, with cafés and boutiques, a new town square and some tasteful decoration. He parked near the bank and, realizing that he was ravenous and still had half an hour till his appointment, found a place to eat. At five minutes before one, with his belly full, the adrenalin running and spoiling for a confrontation, he was leaving the café when he suddenly thought, *God, I'm actually pumped. Giving these people hell is going to feel good. Maybe I'm more like Dad than I knew.*

The bank manager had a corner office, pleasantly appointed, with—yet again—a Walter Lothian seascape prominently displayed. His name was Herb Wilshire, a round-faced forty-year-old with a confident handshake and an annoyingly sincere smile. Seeing Greg's eyes on the painting, he nodded in satisfaction. "Yes, Mr. Lothian, I see you noticed. The bank was sensible enough to purchase that a few years back. At my suggestion, I might add. Not enough businesses support local artists, but it is our policy to try. So let me say, first off, how very sad we were to hear of your father's passing. Also—er—so swiftly, your mother. You have my sincere condolences."

Greg wasn't taken in for a moment. The guy obviously knew full well why he was here, and was trying to soften the ground in advance. That wasn't going to work, and Greg was determined to waste no time with niceties. "Thank you," he said coldly. "However, I think you should know that I hold this institution at least partly responsible for what happened to my parents."

Herb Wilshire's smile vanished. "I don't understand."

"I think that very probably you do, but I'll spell it out, anyway.

You must be aware that my parents were conned out of a large sum of money and that it was stolen from their account at this bank?"

The manager looked at Greg speculatively. "Yes, I did know that."

"Some criminal phoned my mother, pretended to be what he called an 'account inspector,' tricked her into revealing her secret information and then looted the account of twenty thousand dollars." Greg produced the passbook and tossed it across the manager's desk. "It's all documented there."

Wilshire flipped open the passbook with one finger, glanced at it briefly, then switched his attention to his computer, rapidly tapping at the keys. Greg could not see the result, but the other man studied the screen, chewed on his lip, then looked sharply at Greg. "Mr. Lothian, are you familiar with the term *vishing*?"

"Vishing? What's that?"

"Well, you must know about *phishing*, where fraud artists set up a phony website to mimic the site of—say—this bank, and then, by e-mail, con their victims into logging onto that site and divulging their account information?"

"I've heard of it."

"Vishing is the same thing, but it's done over the phone. The word stands for *voice phishing*. Instead of using a bogus website, the crook pretends to personally represent the institution—the phony account inspector that you mentioned—and get the information that way. That's likely how your parents were tricked, which is understandable."

Greg's anger rose a notch. "Understandable?"

Wilshire nodded, apparently oblivious to the effect of his cool appraisal. "Unfortunately, many people, especially those who are older and—how shall I say—less financially astute, are all too easily taken in by this modern brand of grifting. Of course, the bank continually cautions its customers against divulging any of their account and personal information. We post the warnings online and . . ." he slid a printed form in Greg's direction, "mail them out regularly, along with the bank statements. But our best efforts are sometimes ignored, so that all the safeguards the bank has taken such care to institute are useless."

"But why," Greg interrupted, "would my parents have been targeted in the first place?"

"That's a mystery." Wilshire frowned speculatively. "It's possible that someone got hold of a bank statement, perhaps by going through their trash, or stealing their mail. That'd certainly give them all the information they needed to start a confidence trick. But, I'll be frank, it wouldn't have worked if your mother hadn't been so trusting. And when folks are taken in this manner, I must tell you that some people believe that the bank would be justified in disclaiming responsibility."

"What kind of heartless crap is that?" Greg all but snarled. "You've no idea how important that money was to my parents. No damn notion at all."

"Mr. Lothian," Wilshire said calmly. "It's our assumption that *all* of our clients' resources are vital: as important as our duty to protect them. That's why, when ignorance, or even negligence, has enabled the committing of a crime, we still protect our customers."

"What's that supposed to mean?"

"It means that if we're satisfied there has been no malfeasance on the account holder's part, it is our policy to reimburse what has been stolen. The bank takes the loss, not the client."

Greg stared. "Are you saying you're prepared to replace my parents' money?"

"I'm saying it's already been done."

The manager turned his computer. With a hollow sensation, Greg peered at the screen. There it was, the current month of his parents' savings account. The only difference from the passbook was the final entry—a credit of twenty thousand dollars. After his first shock, Greg pulled himself together enough to note the entry date, at last unable to avoid the awful truth: on that last night—perhaps even as early as when his father was still alive—the money that had caused all the trouble had already been restored.

"Why?" he whispered at last.

"Why replace the money?"

"Why didn't you let them *know*?"

"I'm sure we did. The clerk would have made it clear that it was possible. Perhaps, at the time, your mother was too distraught to understand. Anyway, the next account statement would have shown . . . Mr. Lothian, are you all right?"

Greg heard a buzzing in his ears. His vision blurred and for a moment he felt as though he might faint. Further anxious words from the bank manager seemed to be coming from some distance away. He forced himself to take several deep breaths and the shock symptoms receded. "I'm sorry," he muttered. "This has been a—difficult time."

"Of course. I understand. Can I get you anything? A glass of water?"

"No, no! I'm all right." Greg swayed to his feet, resisting the urge to stare at the telltale figures on the computer screen. "I—should have known that this might happen. It's just a pity that my parents . . . Never mind. I really came in to tell you that—er—I'm the executor of my father's will. When probate is granted, I'll come in again."

Herb Wilshire had risen too. He came around his desk, looking genuinely distressed. "Of course," he said hastily. "But do you need any money now? If you let us make a copy of the will, I can authorize cash for expenses, even before probate."

"No, that's fine. I'm fine. Everything's—fine. Thanks for your help. Goodbye."

Then, with very little memory of the journey between, Greg found himself in his car, driving back along Riverbottom Road.

When he got to the house, he did not turn in, but kept on going, driving absent-mindedly, until the road turned onto the Old Lake

Cowichan Road, which in turn joined the new highway, eventually ending up at the lake itself. Beyond the village at the south end, there was a waterside park, which he arrived at by chance, ending his blind journey when the road stopped at the water.

He sat in the car at the lakeside, facing a grand panorama of lake and forested mountains, seeing nothing, his mind still reeling at the implications of all that had happened. He couldn't decide which was worse: the theft of the money, causing the chain of circumstances that had resulted in two deaths, or the sickening irony of the funds having been replaced, but too late. The bank—no doubt backed by insurance—had reimbursed the twenty grand with what amounted to alacrity, the tragedy being that somehow their intentions had not been understood. Yet they couldn't have foreseen the repercussions. No one could. What had occurred was purely unpredictable, with no one directly to blame.

Yet the sequence *had* required a specific trigger: not a real actor this time, but an anonymous cipher, a concocted persona whose very title was a brazen lie—the account inspector.

As Greg sat in solitude, trying to wring some sense out of the confusion that had taken over his life, it began to appear that everything despicable had at its core the kind of heartless evil that had led to the conning and ultimate death of his parents.

"One day!" Greg murmured, oblivious to everything but the rage that now seemed to have taken up permanent residence in his heart. "*One day . . .!*"

NINE

"Goodness, Greg," his sister said. "Are you okay?"

"What do you mean?"

"You sound odd. Almost like you've been drinking."

Greg laughed dryly into the phone. "Very perceptive. I've been into Dad's Scotch, if you must know. He left quite a supply."

"Well, good for you. Are you staying at the house?"

"For a day or two, till I get stuff organized. I found Dad's will, by the way."

"What does it say?"

"It's surprisingly clear and simple. Mum being gone, everything passes to us equally. I'm named as executor. Is that okay with you?"

"Of course. Dad didn't approve of either of us much, but at least he knew how painfully honest you are."

"Painful being the operative word, eh?"

"That's not what I meant. Look—I'm sorry I haven't been over. After Mum—did what she did—there didn't seem to be much point. That was shocking, but I guess I'm not completely surprised."

He hadn't told Jill about his recent discoveries—not the cancer, not the bank fraud, not any of the tangled web that had led to their parents' deaths. It was so sordid and sad, it was hard to imagine telling it to anyone. Perhaps Jill had a right to know, or maybe she'd be happier in the dark. He was still too disturbed and angry to decide about that.

Her last words, however, made him wonder if perhaps she'd suspected more than he knew. "Oh?" he replied. "Why would you say that?"

"Well, we both know how they were—Dad wrapped up in his damn painting and Mum wrapped up in him. Let's be honest, when we left home, they probably hardly even noticed. So, after Dad up and died unexpectedly, I can see Mum thinking she had nothing else to live for and—you know—just wanting to follow right along. Don't you see that?"

If only it had been so simple. Yet it was a perfectly plausible explanation, and perhaps better left that way. "I guess so," he said. "Are you planning to come over sometime soon?"

After a small pause, Jill said, "Greg, to tell the truth, I've been pretty snowed under here. And you certainly don't need me to help with the organizing. You're so good at that. So there's just the question of a memorial. Do you think they'd have wanted one?"

"I doubt it. I went out and picked up the ashes, but I've no idea what to do with them. Neither of them were religious, as you know very well. They kept so much to themselves, they hardly had any friends. I can't think of anyone—except the neighbours, the Lynleys. The old guy's dead and Mrs. Lynley's pretty sick, so that just leaves Lucy. You remember Lucy Lynley?"

"Yes. Is she still at home?"

"Came back to look after her mum. She was taking painting lessons from Dad, as a matter of fact."

"Oh. How interesting."

Greg could tell by his sister's tone just now *un*interested she was, and that her mind was rapidly deploying elsewhere. "I'm going to be staying at the house for a while. I've already got a lawyer working on the probate. When that comes through, I'll get busy on the division of assets. I'm going to make a full inventory. You can let me know if you want anything, and we can sell the rest. Am I right in thinking that you don't want to live here at the house?"

"God, no."

"Me neither. I'll get it ready for putting on the market, then. I want everything settled properly. That's the least I can do." He heard his sister chuckle. "What?"

"Nothing," Jill said. "It's just—Greg, you're such an *accountant.*"

"Uptight, you mean?"

"Maybe, but don't think I don't appreciate it. In the business world, you meet so many shysters. It's just good to know that my brother isn't one of them."

After a few more words, his sister bade him farewell. Greg knew he shouldn't be bothered by her description of him: in her Walter-like manner, she was only being frank, and not, in fact, inaccurate. An accountant, after all, was what he was, not just by trade, but in his heart. After he put down the phone, he poured some more whisky and took it into the office, now completely organized. Surveying his handiwork, the sense and good order painstakingly created from the confusion he'd found there, should have given him satisfaction, but he just felt bleak.

The sour feeling, the annoyance and dull sense of injustice that now seemed to be his constant companions, did not divert him from the task at hand. Powerless to control the past, he blocked it out by grimly concentrating on endless detail. He'd told his sister that he was going to inventory their parents' assets, and this he was determined to do, right down to the final paintbrush and the last loonie.

In fact, it turned out to be quite an endeavour. He went over the property from one end to the other, counting, categorizing, estimating worth. The studio took the most time. There were over two hundred paintings, and he listed them all by title, medium and size, estimating their provisional value by contacting several galleries. Much of the rest of the stuff was worthless, fodder for the Salvation Army or the dump, but he included it anyway, finding first relief and then a mild pleasure in the simple routine. Having always found solace in wrestling numbers, he discovered that this extended naturally to the organization of belongings. Granted, these were the leavings of parents whose only use for him—it seemed in meaner moments—was that he clean up their mess. But in doing this, he discovered a kind of retroactive connection, if not closeness, to those two. By the end of a week of steady labour, helped along by evening infusions of Glenfiddich, he had completed the task.

On Monday, nine days after he'd picked up his parents' ashes, he knew it was time to get back to town. He'd taken two weeks off work, so there were still a few days before he needed to return. But there was a lot to do, including a decision about renewing his apartment lease, a detail which recent events had pushed right out of his mind. Still, as he drove over the Malahat Range into Victoria, glimpsing from the summit the familiar vista of ocean and islands in the bright morning sun, he felt remarkably cheerful. It seemed that he was at last emerging from the protracted period of anxiety and gloom.

By the time he reached Oak Bay Avenue, with his neat apartment block in sight, he was so revived that he found that, subconsciously, he'd already made a decision: hell, the extra money for rent wasn't going to break him. He'd renew the lease on the new terms, and that would be one less thing to think about.

He parked the car in his spot, entered the building from the rear and stopped off in the lobby to pick up his mail. His box wasn't large, and he hadn't checked it for several days prior to moving to the Cowichan Valley, so it was likely to be pretty full. That in mind, he opened the door carefully, ready to catch anything that might fall—but there was nothing to catch. The box was empty.

Surprised, Greg immediately thought that he must have opened the wrong box. But a quick check of the number put that idea to rest; it was his box all right. Yet somehow, in almost two weeks, he appeared to have received no mail at all.

This oddity was not enough to dampen his recovered spirits, but it did add to the feeling of being slightly less than at home as he took the elevator. Entering his apartment, he was aware of the dank smell that abandonment had produced. He went immediately to open the balcony door, thinking as he did so that the place seemed smaller, no doubt the effect of spending nine days rattling around in his parents' big old barn.

Crossing to his bedroom, he noticed that the light on the old telephone answering machine was blinking. That was another oddity, since he rarely used his landline. He'd only kept it connected because, despite using his cell almost exclusively, he wasn't quite ready to cut free from the old ways. Whoever had called on the landline must have got his number from the book.

Intrigued, Greg examined the machine. He hadn't used it in so long that it took a moment to find the "play messages" button. He located it at last and pressed, and the message emerged loud and clear:

Mr. Lothian, this is Malcolm Spender from Island Electronics. The cheque you tendered for the flat-screen TV you purchased last week has been returned NSF. Please contact the store as soon as you get this message. This is Tuesday. If we have not heard from you by the end of the week, the matter will be put in the hands of the authorities. Thank you.

TEN

"I don't understand," Greg said. "I'm Greg Lothian, but I've never been in this store before, let alone bought a TV here."

He was standing in the showroom of Island Electronics, a small establishment on Fort Street which he hadn't known existed till an hour before. The man he confronted, who was not the Malcolm Spender of the phone message, did not seem impressed. He fetched a file from the office and opened it to produce an invoice and a cancelled cheque with the letters NSF stamped in red. "This is your name, isn't it, sir? And your address?"

Flabbergasted, Greg looked at the cheque. The name and address were certainly his. The signature even looked something like his own. But the bank was one he'd never used in his life.

The cheque was for twenty-seven hundred dollars.

"This is ludicrous," he breathed. "This isn't my cheque. I don't have an account at that bank. What in the hell is going on?"

The clerk shrugged, then looked beyond Greg to another man approaching. "Hey, Malc," he called, "the bum cheque guy's here."

"I tell you I'm *not*—" Greg began, but was cut off by the newcomer.

"Who are *you*?" Malc demanded.

"I told you," the first clerk said. "It's Lothian—the guy who ripped us with that dud cheque."

"I didn't," Greg snapped.

"He's not," Malc added. "This isn't the man who bought the TV. This isn't Lothian at all."

It took a long time, a stack of ID and several phone calls, but at last the facts of the matter were sorted out. Greg was the victim of fraud. He couldn't think how it had happened—and then he remembered: the theft of his wallet from the gas station. That's what must have done it. He'd cancelled his credit cards and replaced his driver's licence, but the documentation in the stolen wallet—including, of course, his Social Insurance card—had been more than enough for identity theft. That possibility might even have occurred to him, had not the other troubles erupted in his life.

Bearing the phony cheque, Greg hurried to the bank where the account had been set up by his bogus alter-ego. After a rigmarole that was becoming sickeningly familiar, his true identity was established and the account cancelled. In Greg's opinion, the people at the bank could have been more sympathetic. Their only advice was that he inform the police, which was the next stop on his agenda anyway.

Detective Sergeant Mike Tremblay, of the Victoria City Police Fraud Squad, was a large, amiable man with a ginger buzz cut and pale, shrewd eyes. Greg got in to see him early the same afternoon. Though patient and civil, Tremblay was not exactly overwhelmed by his plight; obviously, the sergeant had heard the identical lament a thousand times before.

"I'm sorry, Mr. Lothian," he said, "but you must realize that there's not much we can do at this point. Now that we have your details, we'll add them to our data bank, of course. When you're contacted by other people who've been scammed in your name—and you will be, believe me—you can refer them to us. We do catch these crooks from time to time. And if your ID comes up when we bust someone, we'll let you know. Apart from that, all I can say is I'm sorry. And next time, be more careful of your wallet."

Greg knew that he should have expected no more than this, but he was annoyed nonetheless, so much so that he found himself blurting out—if only to make this guy just a little more understanding—the story of what had happened to his parents. When he finished, his only reward was a brief shake of the head.

"Yeah, that's tough, Mr. Lothian," Detective Tremblay said. "It seems your family has been having a really bad time lately. When this sort of thing happens, people are always hurt and amazed, and the question I'm most often asked is, why we don't do more to stop it. Well, sir, it's a hard and tricky world. From where I stand, it's getting rougher all the time, what with drugs and guns and gangs—yeah, even here in Victoria—and, of course, the damn Internet, which is the biggest gift to the rogue element since the invention of money. And although we're working harder than ever to contain them, to be honest, it's only on my best days that I feel we're even keeping even. You've obviously had some bad experiences, Mr. Lothian, but sadly, I hear your kind of story every day. If I had more men, better resources, ten times the budget for public information programs, not to mention police overtime, things might be better. But, frankly, even that's a damn big *if*."

Frustrated, Greg shook his head. "What am I supposed to do now?"

"Keep your wits about you, and your eye on your wallet," the detective smiled bleakly, "and get over it."

When he arrived home at the apartment, it was nearly 5:00. He'd wasted most of an entire day patching up the shredded mess of his life. By habit, he checked the mail, again finding nothing. Then, with a flash of understanding that almost made him nauseous, he tumbled to the obvious: this abrupt and unexplained lack had to be connected with the theft of his identity. How it could have been done, or exactly why, he didn't know, but it was pretty clear that someone was stealing his mail.

If that was the case, however, it was too late in the day to do anything about it. Fuming, he went upstairs and started to make supper; then he realized that what he wanted was a good stiff belt of Glenfiddich. Since he'd only acquired the taste, there was none in the apartment, but feeling as he did, he was damned if that was going to stop him. There was a liquor store a block away on Oak Bay Avenue. Suspending his supper preparations, Greg left the apartment almost at a trot, on an errand that recently would have seemed shocking to him.

But though the whisky did its soothing work, it also seemed out of place in his own home, vaguely distasteful and perhaps even cowardly. Confining himself to one decent-sized drink and a smaller follow-up, he ate supper, then made a pot of coffee and turned on his computer.

What he realized was that he knew far too little about the sort of crime that had come calling on his parents, and now himself. Oh, he'd seen reports in the newspaper and on TV about theft and fraud of all kinds, but he hadn't paid attention. Secure in his careful and complacent world, he'd always felt above such distasteful matters, a naïve notion that a double dose of grim reality had suddenly shattered. Detective Tremblay had seemed to regard the Internet as just one more irritant that criminals used to make his life harder. What he had not added was that the same instrument could be a source of protection. Greg intended to use it to bring himself up to date so he could begin, at last, to live in the real world.

With his PC fired up, he went to Google and in the search window typed "Identity Theft." The result was amazing. Literally thousands of websites were listed, the first few of which provided so much information that Greg didn't stir from the screen until after midnight.

Having familiarized himself with the overall picture, he then concentrated specifically on mail theft. It was depressingly easy: stolen ID was used to have the owner's mail forwarded to another address. Bank statements then provided access to account numbers; pre-approved credit-card offers could be accepted and used to build up massive debt; personal information was fodder for an array of criminal activities—all in the victim's name. Should there be any cheques or cash in the mail, that was just a bonus.

Of course, now that he suspected what had happened, he could alert the post office right away, but that wouldn't stop the thieves from using the information they had already gained, nor would it be much help in catching them. As soon as mail ceased being forwarded, they'd know they'd been rumbled and move on. In cases Greg read about online, one fact was always made clear: when the post office received notification of a bogus forwarding, it was their policy not to reveal the false address. This was probably intended to prevent irate dupes from taking the law into their own hands. Which was all very well and good but, assuming the information went to law enforcement, what could *they* do? Very little, if Greg's meeting with Sergeant Tremblay was any guide. To be fair, fake addresses were usually box numbers, nearly impossible to monitor.

The only thing that made Greg pause during his online exploration was the urge to refresh his drink: as the night wore on, the notion of whisky in his apartment didn't seem quite so distasteful. But the liquor didn't dull his concentration; if anything, it made it more intense. And by the end of the night, when the information had soaked in and the initial distress somewhat abated, he was left with two basic certainties: first, more than anything, he desired the bastard who'd callously stolen his life—his own personal "account inspector"—to be caught; second, no one in any official capacity was likely to be much help in this endeavour.

At 12:30 he turned off the computer and collapsed into bed. The Scotch he'd drunk did provide the blessing of instant oblivion.

Some time later he jerked awake, his head almost exploding with the shock of a new realization. Of course! The theft of his identity and the scam on his parents were connected. According to the bank manager, the older Lothians had been targeted because someone had got hold of their personal information. What better source than the tax package Mary Lothian had sent to him? It hadn't arrived because, along with the rest of Greg's mail, it had been intercepted. This meant that the crooks who'd stolen his ID and those who'd scammed his parents were probably one and the same.

Ever since Greg had found his mailbox empty, the truth had been staring him in the face. Now he had to face an even more uncomfortable fact: the catalyst of it all had been his own carelessness. If he hadn't lost his wallet, none of this would have happened.

Greg slept no more that night. Bitterness and outrage consumed him as, over and over, he went through the events of the last weeks, but his worst reaction was terrible guilt. His mind became prey to such dark thoughts that, by the time dawn was showing through the curtains, he thought he might be going crazy.

It was then, in response to desperation or just by dumb luck, that he had his extraordinary idea.

ELEVEN

Greg arrived at his local post office branch at opening time, with his story well rehearsed. Although he had arranged to have his mail forwarded several weeks ago—so went the tale—there was one important letter that didn't seem to have arrived at the new destination. At this point he wasn't sure if it hadn't been sent, or if he *had* received it at his original address but, in the flurry of moving, misplaced it. So he had just one question: would it be possible to check the actual date on which he'd arranged to have the forwarding begin?

The clerk was a pleasant young woman who, after checking his ID, noting the old address on his driver's licence—but not, luckily, asking for details of the new one—went out back to check the records. So far, so good. His strategy now was straightforward: in the slim chance that there was no record of a forwarding order, he'd know he'd been mistaken about mail theft, but if a date *was* provided, then he'd be sure his fears were correct.

In a couple of minutes, the clerk returned. With a smile, she wrote something on a piece of paper and slid it across to him. "There we are, Mr. Lothian. Is that what you need?"

Greg looked at the paper. What was written was a date three weeks previously. "Yes. Thanks very much."

"You're welcome. I hope it helps you find that letter."

Greg nodded, trying not to show his elation. In this brief

operation, he had achieved two objectives: he was now certain that his mail was being stolen, and he'd found this out without disturbing the operation. "Thank you," he said quietly. "I'm sure it'll help me one way or another."

Feeling almost like a con artist himself, Greg left the post office.

The idea that had come to him at the end of his long, sleepless night was so simple, he was amazed it had taken so long. Stripped down, it amounted to this: since it was impossible, or at best impractical, to track the criminals, the answer was to lure them into the open. The perfect instrument for this was the very thing that was causing so much trouble: the mail. This could be turned around, made into a trap. All he needed was the right bait.

Greg went home and thought about it all day. While doing so, he cleaned and tidied his apartment, letting his mind quietly pick away at all the possibilities and permutations. However the trap turned out, it should not involve this apartment: that would be too dangerous, and it was also unlikely that the thief could be lured here. Also, whatever plan *did* emerge, it should be set in motion soon: if the mail forwarding was allowed to continue too long, that in itself could provoke suspicion.

Around suppertime, he got an urge for a Scotch. Pouring from his newly acquired—and expensive—bottle reminded him of the still-substantial stash at his parents' house, and then the next piece of the puzzle fell into place. Of course! Isolated Riverbottom Road was the perfect location for his trap.

By mid-evening, he'd also figured out the bait.

Dear Greg,

I hope you are managing to cope with the sudden death of our parents. I'm afraid that this week it really has been preying on my mind, especially since my bad back has made it impossible for me to do anything much but lie around. Neither of us were very close to Mum and Dad, I know, so I'm surprised how much I seem to be missing the old dears. Do you think we should hold the memorial in Duncan? If so, it shouldn't be for at least a month or so, when hopefully I'm more able to get around.

It's good of you to do all the clearing up at the old place. I wish I could help, but the doctor says I must rest. You're terribly busy, which means you'll only be able to get up from Victoria on weekends. That doesn't matter, of course, even if it takes till the end of summer to clear out the house for selling. But unfortunately, Riverbottom Road is such an isolated location that, should word get out that the house is unoccupied, it'd be easy for thieves to ransack it undisturbed. I don't know if people going by on the Cowichan River can see that there's no one there. I sure hope not. But there's one thing I think you should see to right away. Remember that little safe in Dad's studio, where he used to keep the money when he sold pictures for cash, to avoid declaring the income for taxes? I don't know if you realized, but as recently as last Christmas, the old fox had thousands of dollars in there. You should check that out right away and get the money in the bank. Everything else can be done at leisure. Maybe in a while, when I'm feeling better, I can help.

Meanwhile, Greg, thanks for everything you've done, and for being so understanding. I hope that when you've got the time, you'll pay your useless old sis a visit up here in Nanaimo. We haven't seen each other much lately, but I do miss you.

Love, Jill

When he'd finished writing the letter on the computer, working on it till it seemed just right, he found some notepaper and a pen, and copied it out laboriously, using a round hand he'd been taught in grade school and had hardly used since. When it was complete, he reread it several times, trying to imagine himself a stranger looking at this thing for the first time. Was all the necessary information clear enough?

Was it sufficiently woven into the text to look believable? The one thing he wasn't certain about was his reference to the house's location. Should he have included the street number? If the mail thieves were the villains who had conned his parents, they'd have the address anyway, and that would prove the connection. Of course, should it be a different set of criminals, he was in trouble. But, so sure was he, he was willing to risk it. All the other information in the letter—save the existence of the safe and the money—was accurate, right up to his sister's name. He'd included that, plus some feeling of the true family situation, in an attempt to make the letter seem more real. Jill wasn't ill and didn't live in Nanaimo, but they probably wouldn't check on that. Nanaimo, however, was where he intended to mail the letter, first thing tomorrow.

Satisfied, he placed the note in an envelope, addressing it to himself in the same round hand. He sealed it, put on a stamp and laid it on the kitchen table, ready to go. He freshened his drink, returning to stare in satisfaction at the tasty morsel of bait, so judiciously fashioned. He had to admit it looked good, truly authentic, and it struck him that this was a work of considerable craft and imagination. He'd always thought of himself as a pedestrian sort of fellow, short on creativity, the antithesis of the artistic personality. Yet what he'd produced was, in its way, as clever as anything his father had made. Also, this had a very practical—not to mention just—purpose. Would the old man have been capable of coming up with such a trick? He wasn't sure. When forced to acknowledge unpleasant realities, all Walter Lothian had ever exhibited was rage—the thing that ultimately had been his undoing.

But he had sure had good taste in whisky.

TWELVE

It was Thursday morning when Greg drove the 110 kilometres north to Nanaimo. Originally a mining town, Nanaimo had in recent years blossomed into a vibrant community, with modern shops, condos and parks clustered around a beautiful harbour. A bypass highway had restored relative tranquility to the town centre, and Greg reached it without effort by late morning to do his mailing.

Afterward, he had a feeling of anticlimax. The letter wouldn't reach Victoria until the next day, and, assuming the fake forwarding address was somewhere in that city, delivery wouldn't be until Monday. If it was read promptly and the bait swallowed, the earliest a response could be expected was later that day. In Greg's present mood, it seemed like an eternity until then.

Driving south again on the Trans-Canada, a highway that seemed to get busier every year, he began to realize that he was actually fortunate to have a few days to get his act together. Though he'd selected a good location and created admirable bait, he did not as yet have a real trap, or even a concrete plan. To set these up was going to take all the time he had.

Reaching Duncan, midway in the journey home, he considered taking a detour to his parents' house, then decided against it. The first priority was to get things settled in Victoria. He reached the city in the early afternoon, not going home, but straight to his office.

His boss, George Allrod, the senior partner in the accountancy firm, was a pleasant, mild man, a few years short of retirement. Greg had always got along well with him; in fact, the last time they'd talked, just prior to the beginning of the troubles, George had hinted at the imminent offer of a partnership. That was all very fine, but what Greg wanted right now was some more time off.

"Of course, take whatever you need," George said, in answer to Greg's request. "You're one of my best people, Greg, and I'm happy to help any way I can. It's because of what happened with your family, I take it?"

"That's right."

"I'm so sorry about that. An awful thing to have both parents pass so suddenly."

"One led to the other, I'm afraid."

George nodded his graying head sympathetically. "Yes, so I'd heard. It's terribly sad. Sometimes, it seems, people feel they just can't carry on without their partner. Hard for those who are left behind though. How are you holding up?"

"As well as can be . . . you know."

"I understand. But, come to think of it . . ."

"What?"

"It doesn't matter."

"Tell me."

"In the short time we've been talking, I've been feeling a little surprised."

"By what?"

"*You*, in fact. I know our line of work is supposed to a bit sober, and I guess we are, compared to some professions, anyway. And you've always been a sort of poster boy for that idea."

"Do you think so?"

"Absolutely. Ever since I've known you, you've been so reserved. But now, today, despite your loss, or maybe because of it, you seem—how can I put it?—somehow more *alive* than I can remember."

"Really?"

George laughed in sudden embarrassment. "But what do I know, eh? I'm just rattling on. All that matters is that you have the sympathy of everyone here. So, as I said, take whatever time you need. And we'll look forward to seeing you back as soon as you're ready."

From work, Greg headed home to Oak Bay. Entering his apartment, he encountered the now-familiar sensation of being a stranger, and this time he had an extra thought: perhaps he wouldn't renew that lease after all. But he was too preoccupied to take the notion further than that. His purpose in returning was only to pick up some clothes in preparation for a longer stay in the house by the river.

While he was packing, the conversation with his boss kept coming back into his mind. That last observation George had made: Greg wasn't sure whether he should be flattered or insulted. Certainly the new feeling, now a constant companion, of strange and dangerous things happening just out of sight, was enough to keep anyone pretty damned alert. If this came across as extra aliveness, so be it. He'd make sure to use the sensation to hone his concentration, not to mention patience and cunning, for the task ahead.

"Alive?" he muttered grimly, as he packed the last of his things and headed to the car. "George, you don't know the half of it."

He arrived back at the old house in the late afternoon. In consternation, he saw smoke coming from the studio chimney, then he remembered Lucy Lynley. He'd told her to continue using the place, so she must have taken him at his word. To his further surprise, he found that the thought of the young woman working away in the domain his father had once ruled felt mysteriously pleasant.

The studio door was ajar. He entered quietly to discover Lucy hard at work, her back turned, at the far end of the studio. Only after he was in the room did he realize that she was unaware of him. He gave a cough, whereupon she shrieked and dropped her paintbrush. She whirled to face him, then gave her friendly laugh and blushed. "Sorry—I didn't know anyone was here."

"No, *I'm* sorry," Greg replied. "I only just arrived. I didn't mean to startle you."

"That's okay," Lucy retrieved the brush and began to clean it off. "I should be finishing up anyway."

"Please don't leave on my account. I said you were welcome to use the studio anytime." This was true, but even as he spoke, he knew that soon her visits would have to be curtailed. From next Monday, the property must appear to be unoccupied, according to his plan to turn it into a trap. So he was going to have to come up with a plausible story.

"Thanks," Lucy was saying, "but I must be getting back to Mum."

"Okay, whatever you think." He watched as she finished cleaning up. The painting she'd been working on was different from the one his mother had brought him to see, what seemed an age ago. He'd liked that one, but this was better, again an airy landscape, but with more strength and authority in the brushwork. More startling, however, was the discovery that he understood this. He heard himself saying, "I'm going to be staying at the house for a while."

"Oh, good," Lucy replied casually. "Then perhaps we'll see more of you." She finished her cleaning, wiped her hands and paused at the door. "Listen, if you're not busy, why not come over tomorrow evening for supper? I know Mum would love to see you again."

It was in his mind to refuse. Then he realized that it would be as good a time as any to gently persuade Lucy to make herself scarce for a while; he'd have to think up a good excuse, but this gave him a day to think about it. "Thank you," he said. "If you're sure it's not too much trouble."

They continued making polite conversation, and then she left briskly. Catching himself wishing that the departure had not been quite so abrupt, he thought, *This is ridiculous; she's just a neighbour. Get it together, for God's sake.*

He fetched his bag from the car and went into the house, in search of a shot of Glenfiddich.

THIRTEEN

Next morning, after breakfast, Greg walked the property, trying to see it from the perspective of an intruder. The first thing any respectable thief would do, he imagined, would be to thoroughly check the place out. The only way the house could be found was by the street address. (The number on the gatepost was partially obscured by greenery: one detail that needed immediate attention.) This part of Riverbottom Road was quite lonely, and no houses were visible from the gate. It would be easy to park unobtrusively nearby and walk in. For Greg, therefore, the first priority was to decide on a spot for surveillance. He chose a garden shed a short distance from the house, with a window that gave a good view of all approaches and enough room inside to set up a long-term operation.

The location of the house was a double-edged sword; isolation gave what seemed like safe access for a burglar, but it also made it easy to quietly close the trap behind him. Once the house was entered, all Greg needed to do was phone the police from his place of concealment and the thief could be apprehended before he knew what was happening.

For the rest of the morning, Greg wandered the house and the property, going over details, examining all angles. If the robber arrived at night—the most likely scenario—the darkness could be a real problem; even in the close proximity of the garden shed, he might miss a stealthy approach. If the front courtyard light was left on, its usual state, it might make an intruder nervous, but it would also show that the courtyard was empty of vehicles, a usually reliable indicator of unoccupied houses. The Prius, of course, would be well hidden.

But even with sufficient light, it would still be well nigh impossible for one person to pay undivided attention to the house over a prolonged vigil. Some sort of alarm was required to give an alert, night or day. Greg had a solid, practical streak, so after mulling over the problem for a while, he arrived at a solution, low-tech but workable. The Canadian Tire store in Duncan provided all the materials, and by the end of the day, Greg had his warning device. It consisted of a spring-loaded switch attached to a tree in a part of the driveway that could not be avoided by anyone coming in from the road. A well-concealed wire ran through the woods to a small, battery-powered buzzer in the garden shed. The switch on the tree was kept in the "off" position by a near-invisible thread, stretched under tension across the driveway at mid-calf level. If that thread was broken, the switch was automatically activated and the buzzer came on in the shed. Voila!

Greg tested his device several times; it worked perfectly. His satisfaction was such that when he at last finished up and went inside, he found himself chuckling. It was early evening, time for a well-deserved whisky. He was just starting to pour when he remembered his supper invitation from Lucy.

As he approached along the river path, a black shape shot out of the woods, nearly bowling him over. Lucy's Lab, Hatch—he surprised himself by recalling the name—was as enthusiastic as ever, licking and nuzzling and falling over him all the way to the Lynleys' door. Lucy chuckled when she saw them together. "Hello. I might have known. Down, Hatch. He seems to like you. I hope the idiot hasn't mauled you too badly. Come in."

Greg entered, followed by Hatch, who was allowed in this time.

Delicious cooking smells wafted on the air as he followed Lucy through the house, making him realize that he hadn't eaten a proper sit-down meal in days. In the living room, Shirl Lynley was propped comfortably, a glass of wine beside her, looking, he thought, less frail than before. She greeted Greg warmly, telling her daughter to pour him wine, which she was already doing. Soon, with Shirl surveying him benignly, and Lucy popping in and out from the kitchen as she completed dinner preparations, Greg was almost able to forget the dark purposes that had been consuming him.

Supper was a simple but well-cooked meal of roast chicken and vegetables, preceded by squash soup and followed by a fruit crumble, both homemade. Lucy opened another bottle of wine, topping up Greg's glass when it was emptied, which seemed to happen quite frequently. He was surprised; a single glass of wine had traditionally been quite enough for him. His recent introduction to whisky appeared to be bringing about some changes. But he didn't care. He felt good. And when, after supper, Shirl Lynley said goodnight and was helped to bed, he was even happier to be left alone with her daughter.

When Lucy returned and poured him yet another glass of wine, they began to talk about painting: specifically, how it was that with such a talented and famous father, Greg had felt so alienated from his world. "Even back when we were kids," Lucy said, "I remember you hated anything to do with art. Once I actually heard you yell that at your dad. He was so mad. And I was shocked, because normally you hardly said boo to a goose. Have you any idea what made you dislike something your dad was so passionate about?"

Greg grinned crookedly. "Him! The old man himself! I disliked it *because* he cared about it. My only way of getting back at him. Pretty childish, I guess."

"But understandable. Your dad certainly could be a fierce old general. Never quite stopped, I'm afraid."

"Which brings up something I've always wondered. How come

you were never scared of him? He had our whole family under his thumb, but not you."

Lucy pursed her lips in thought. "I'd like to say it was because my own folks were so easy-going, but it was more than that. Even as a kid, I seemed somehow to understand that if you didn't take his bluster seriously, if you didn't let him ride you, he usually calmed down. That's part of it. But also—it's hard to put this into words—in some odd way our particular personalities just seemed to—*fit*."

Lucy started to blink and Greg realized there were tears in her eyes. "Oh, man," he said quickly. "I'm sorry."

"It's okay," she replied. "I don't think I realized until now how much I miss him. He wasn't so much *teaching* me painting, you know, as . . ."

"What?"

"Letting me grow into it, working in his studio, surrounded by his stuff. Letting it demonstrate what could be done, but allowing me to be free to take my own direction."

"No kidding!"

"You're amazed, of course. Knowing Walter, who wouldn't be. But I think he was changing. Doing his best to, anyway. Maybe, in some odd way, he was even trying to make up for how he'd been with his own family, driving you and Jill away like he did."

"He *told* you that?"

"Goodness no!" Lucy chuckled. "I said I thought there'd been a change, not a miracle. The thing about why you and Jill left, I got from your mum. Poor Mary might not have been able to stand up to Walter, but she knew perfectly well what had happened with her children. It wasn't her fault, but she blamed herself anyway, and I know for sure that it broke her heart."

Hearing Lucy speak of his mother that way brought back everything that had happened so powerfully that he was shocked by her death all over again. He turned away, feeling an almost overwhelming urge to blurt out everything that had been going on: the foul trickery behind his parents' demise; his rage at the architects of their misery and his own; the plot he was hatching in revenge. All the indignation and hurt, dammed up so long, threatened to burst through and make him spill everything. A moment more and his tongue would start babbling. Not only would his secret be out, but he would likely as not scare the wits out of Lucy, something that was not to be considered.

The only way to prevent this catastrophe, he knew, was to get out of there fast. "I'm sorry, Lucy," he muttered. "I can't talk about this anymore tonight. It's getting late and I should go."

If Lucy was surprised by the sudden change, she didn't show it. "Of course. I understand. I'm sorry if I spoke out of turn."

"No, no," he said hastily. "What you said was wonderful. You obviously knew both Mum and Dad better than either Jill or I did. I'm grateful for everything you did for them. At the end, it was a lot more than I did, that's for sure."

She argued about that, and they sparred gently a few moments longer, trading compliments and reassurances, until, amidst a final round of thanks and farewells, he managed to extricate himself.

For much of the walk home, he was trailed by the companionable shadow of Hatch. The animal left him at the border of the property. Only then did Greg remember that in his haste to depart, a vital purpose had been left undone: he had not taken steps to keep Lucy away from his trap.

FOURTEEN

By Sunday, the rest of the preparations were complete. Having built the alarm, Greg prepared the garden shed for what was likely to be a long period of surveillance. This hiding place could be regarded essentially as a blind, the wildlife to be spied upon being human, subspecies criminal, and it needed careful preparation. To that end, he stocked it with food, drink, a comfortable chair, reading and writing material and his iPod.

He paid particular attention to his cellphone: this, after all, was the single most important element in his plan, vital for contacting the authorities once the intruder was spotted, so he made sure to test it. From the shed, he phoned several numbers in Duncan and was promptly connected, so that would be no problem. His cell battery was good for days at a charge, but to make doubly sure, he ran an extension cord from the house for his cell charger and the iPod, plus any other power needs that might arise. He also took another trip into town, purchasing a couple of good flashlights, a small plug-in night-light, a big Thermos bottle, food and coffee—everything necessary for a long siege. He was in business.

But he still hadn't warned off Lucy. On Sunday afternoon, when he caught sight of her heading in the direction of the studio, he knew he could delay no longer. He followed her inside, where she was setting up for work. He had decided upon a story and started in right away.

"Hey, Lucy," he said cheerfully, "good to see you again. And thanks for the other night."

Lucy smiled over her easel. "You're welcome. I hope talking about your parents didn't upset you too much."

"No. I was a bit tired, is all. Look, speaking of them—well, of my dad—I was just on the phone to his gallery in Vancouver. They want to arrange a big exhibition and sale. Now that he's, you know, passed on, the interest in his work, not to mention the value, has shot up."

"I'm not surprised."

"But here's the thing: they were very worried about all this priceless work sitting here unguarded. They insisted I lock the place up tight and keep it that way. I've found I have to go back to work sooner than I thought, so I'm going to be leaving tomorrow and I won't be back till I can arrange to have Dad's paintings crated. So I was wondering if you'd mind working at home, just temporarily? I could help you move your stuff, and you could take anything you need. Then, in a couple of weeks, when this has been taken care of, you could come back for as long as you like—or anyway, until the house is sold. What do you say?"

Apparently he was getting good at this trickery thing. The story sounded so plausible that Lucy didn't turn a hair, even offering to stop what she was doing right away. So sweet and reasonable was she that, had the subterfuge not been vital, he would have felt guilty. As it was, he insisted that she stay as long as she liked today, and that he'd help her move, when she was ready.

That evening, after his usual scratched-together supper, sitting alone with a Glenfiddich, the lights bright and CBC playing a concert on the radio, Greg was thinking that on this, the last night of ease before he would go into hiding with his trap loaded and set, he was feeling something which, in other times, might have passed for happy.

FIFTEEN

On Monday morning, Greg shut his parents' old minivan away in the garage, but realized he hadn't decided where to hide the Prius. He settled for parking it out of sight behind the studio, covered by a tarp; should anyone come upon it there, it would merely seem to be in storage. Having closed and locked the house, he retreated to a distance to judge the effect. Yes, the property looked convincingly deserted. Farther up the drive, he reset the switch for his warning buzzer, installing a new thread.

Satisfied, he went back to the garden shed and spent the rest of the day there. Unlikely as it was that anyone would show up so soon, it was safer to be careful. In fact, not even a rabbit stirred during the long hours Greg watched and waited, but that was okay; he figured it was valuable practice.

In the early evening, when it seemed a visitor was least likely to arrive—they'd either come in full light when they could see properly, or in pitch dark to be hidden—Greg retreated to the house. Without putting on any lights, he made supper, used the bathroom, and finished all the preparations for his first night. Then, locking the house again but avoiding the courtyard light, which had come on at dusk, he made a roundabout passage to the shed and settled down.

Just after 1:00 AM, with the buzzer stubbornly silent, his neck stiff and his mind numbed with boredom, he was shocked into alertness—but not by any intruder. His head had fallen forward and cracked painfully against the windowsill. Without warning, he'd fallen dead asleep. He rose to his feet, heart pounding, and, in the glow of a flashlight, poured coffee from his Thermos. Sucking some down cleared his head, but with that came the realization of what he should have known from the start: how could a single person, on permanent vigil, survive without sleep?

Obviously, it was impossible. With no one to spell him, a watcher would sooner or later have to surrender to biology. Greg had no idea when his visitor would arrive, but it might not be for days. If his oh-so-clever plan was to have any chance of success, he'd have to take account of that.

The problem was enough to keep him edgily awake for the rest of the night. But by the time dawn was paling the sky in the direction of Duncan, eclipsing the glow of the courtyard light, which had shone all night on emptiness, he thought he had come up with a solution.

At 5:30 AM he concluded that no one was coming, at that time anyway, so he went into the house. Considering the distance from Victoria, it seemed unlikely that any daytime prowler would arrive until later in the morning. He searched around until he found an old-fashioned alarm clock. When wound and shaken, it began ticking sturdily, and a test of the alarm confirmed that was working too. He had a quick breakfast, then fell into bed.

The alarm clawed him awake at 10:00 AM. Not exactly chipper, but rested, he carefully checked outside to make sure no one had come. Finding everything still and silent, he slipped back to his hiding place to wait out the day.

The mindset that made Greg a good accountant also allowed him to be comfortable with such things as mathematical probability, the law of averages and the random nature of chance. Had he been thinking clearly, rather than involved with the emotion of catching his "account inspector," he would have considered the inevitable need for sleep. Brought to his senses, he now used that logical mind to adjust his plan of action. He had to stop trying to be alert every minute. He must spell himself, aiming to keep guard at the most likely times, doing the best job possible.

That settled, his second day in the shed, Tuesday, passed a lot more pleasantly. Having checked the thread on his warning buzzer, he decided to put his full trust in this first line of defense. Thus he could stop staring numbingly out the window every second of the daylight hours, and take regular naps at night. As long as he didn't become too exhausted, the warning buzzer would wake him if someone approached. Regular sleep periods in the shed could be regulated by the alarm clock, suitably muffled against being heard from outside.

The weather, which had been clear, turned cloudy in the afternoon, with the threat of rain. None arrived, however. At 6:00 PM, Greg went inside for his evening routine. He ate quickly and changed his clothes, keeping a careful eye on the driveway. Stifling the urge for a shot of Glenfiddich, he made a fresh Thermos of coffee. Carrying this and an extra-large mug, he dutifully returned to the shed.

For the next few hours, happy in the knowledge that he could rest when he needed to, he maintained his watch. The image of the big old house, a still photo of ghostly planes and shadows revealed by the courtyard light and later, as the sky cleared, the pale glow of the moon, became etched upon his retina. But still there was no movement. And still there was no sound of the buzzer.

Around midnight, beginning to feel sleepy, Greg set his alarm to go off at 1:00 AM. This was it, the first test. For the next hour, until the alarm wakened him, he was trusting himself to the buzzer. He put out the nightlight and settled back in his chair . . .

And was almost instantly dreaming. From his window, he seemed to see not one but hundreds of intruders, creeping in a dark line toward the house. Horrified, he tried to shout—and started awake, to find that exactly ten minutes had passed.

Grimly, he checked the outside, but of course no one was there. He sat back, relaxing again with surprising ease. The next thing he knew, the alarm was going off. Momentarily mistaking it for the warning buzzer, he felt his heart racing, but that soon passed. He put on the light and poured coffee into the big new mug. His system was working: it was going to be all right.

For the rest of the night, the next day, and the night after that, he continued the same routine. The indignation and rage—not to mention the personal guilt—that had sparked this enterprise did not abate during the long period of waiting. Rather, these emotions were transmuted into a constant background hum of sour resolve, providing nourishment for the near-mystic faith that sooner or later his plan would bear fruit, that the quarry so long awaited would walk at last into the trap.

In fact, it was 2:00 AM on Thursday morning, minutes after he'd woken from his first nap and was pouring coffee, that the silence was finally shattered by the sound of the buzzer.

SIXTEEN

Brrrrrr . . . !!!! Like the whine of a small, vicious insect, the sound split the quiet of the night. Greg was momentarily frozen in shock, then he was clawing at the battery. He found the terminal and wrenched the wire free. Blessed silence, save for the painful echoes in his head.

Fearfully, he hurried to the window. But he knew that the buzzer could not have been heard from outside. Considering the short time it had sounded, confined to the shed and at this distance from the trip-wire, logic told him that it was impossible. What he wasn't prepared for was his own reaction. Abruptly, he'd been transported from the land of fantasy, or at best theory, into a dimension of dreadful reality. He could almost feel the physical presence of the newcomer: a live villain, ruthless and surely dangerous, who'd been lured here by *him*.

Face hot, mouth dry, Greg peered out into the night. The lighted area around the house was as empty as ever. He scanned the courtyard closely from end to end: not a flicker of movement, not the smallest thing out of place.

Nobody.

But then, anyone approaching down the drive, edging along slowly, as an intruder surely must, wouldn't yet have come into sight. They would creep and stop and watch and move on. A careful operator would take a long time, might even . . .

He was there!

At one moment, as Greg's glance slid across the dimly lit courtyard, the area near the front door was unoccupied. Then, as his scan reached the end of its sweep and swung back—it wasn't. As if transported by magic, a lone figure stood statue-still, illuminated by the yard light and the lesser glow of the moon.

Greg drew in a sharp breath, then involuntarily covered his mouth, as if the sound might have been heard. Impossible, of course. The figure remained motionless, its back steadfastly turned, attention entirely on the house.

Nothing happened for more than a minute. Then the figure began to move. Silently, it drifted toward the building. Mesmerized, Greg watched it gain the porch and reach the front door. A flashlight came on, a pinpoint that struck the door handle, then moved to the lock. Greg thought he heard a distant rattle as the handle was tried. Then the light swung around and hovered on a nearby window. Was this where the entry would occur? Would it happen right now? Or was it just a preliminary check, the start of a careful inspection? Obviously the break-in would happen sooner or later, but Greg had to know exactly when it did. He needed the thief to be inside, absorbed in his search, before calling in the law. His intention was to intercept the squad car as it arrived, warning the cops, so they could go in quietly and catch the thief red handed. That was what he'd been waiting for all this time, and he saw that the plan could work. But—once the call was made, the die was cast. If the police came too late, or alerted the suspect, he would escape. No second chances. Everything had to be timed just right.

The light swung away from the window. Staying low, it swept along one side of the house, then the other. The intruder then moved along the porch. Greg's heart sank. According to his bait letter, the safe containing the money was in the studio. But if the thief discovered that first, he would need much less time to understand there was no safe to find.

Greg was just cursing himself for being so specific when the movement on the verandah ceased. The figure stood still, as if in thought, then returned to the front door. There came the tinkle of breaking glass. It was the window that had been examined before, which led into the front hall. The intruder was motionless again, as if listening. Then, with a swift, lithe movement, he disappeared over the sill into the dark.

This was it: the moment Greg had awaited. Presumably, the intruder would now start his search. Since he couldn't know that the studio wasn't part of the main building, it would take him a while to find it. Only then would the hunt begin in earnest for the non-existent safe. Now was the time for that phone call.

Greg pulled out his cell and switched it on. When he saw the lit screen waving around, he realized how much his hand was shaking. The excitement of the hunt was upon him, anticipation buzzing through his body with delicious intensity. With a grunt of concentration, he brought up his hand to punch in the magical numbers: 9–1–1 . . .

But instead of hitting the number pad, he fumbled. His hand jostled the phone, knocking it flying. The instrument did a flip and started to fall. Greg grabbed for it but missed. His eyes followed the lighted screen as it plunged like an Olympic diver, down, down—straight into his coffee mug.

For a second, there was a dull glow from the bottom of the liquid. Then that went out.

Greg gasped in despair. He plunged his hand into the mug, frantically fishing, yanking out the cell. Its heaviness told him, even if the dead screen had not, just how fatal was the news: his lifeline was severed. After all the meticulous preparations, a freak accident had negated his entire plan.

Greg staggered to the shed door and wrenched it open, panting. Sick with shock and frustration, he started at the dark house. Inside, the thief was already moving about, his vile presence violating the place with what now would be impunity.

"Goddamn it!"

The expletive spurted forth like a pistol shot. Greg had no idea if the sound could be heard and didn't care. He wanted to scream his anger at the heavens. The only thing that stopped him was a sick lassitude, which began in his gut and spread through his entire frame. He swayed and almost fell, clutching the door frame. Nearly fainting, he hung there, his breathing low and shallow, until his strength slowly returned.

Bringing with it a desperate idea.

In the house, there was a landline phone. If he could creep in and call the police, without disturbing the intruder, his precious plan might yet be salvaged. It was a wild notion: ridiculous, impossible—terrifying.

And he had to try it.

SEVENTEEN

The house where Greg had grown up, every part of which was safe and utterly familiar, had become an alien entity. Crouched in the gloom, barely revealed by the yard light, it seemed to vibrate with menace.

To approach it directly across the exposed courtyard was out of the question. Carrying his flashlight but using it as little as possible, Greg crept through the woods, heading for the wing on the far left of the house. Here the trees almost touched the building, so there would be cover all the way. From that point, it was but a short distance around the end to the door into the master bedroom. In there was the telephone.

Circling, he kept a nervous eye on the house. Since he was going in, he badly needed some indication of where the intruder was. No sensible burglar would put on lights, even if he thought the place was empty, so his position would likely only be shown by his flashlight. So far, Greg had seen no sign of it.

Then another factor belatedly occurred to him: what if the thief was not alone? What if a lookout was stationed nearby? If so, there was nothing to do but be extra careful, but the idea made him even more nervous and fearful.

Though no less determined.

Apart from tripping and painfully barking his shin at one point, he reached the house without incident. Then he was rewarded: from the window of his old room came a brief flash of light. After his first surprise, Greg paid closer attention. In the window, he made out a distinct glow, varying in intensity as the searcher moved about. Greg gulped in relief: for the moment, at least, he knew the whereabouts of his adversary.

A path led around the end of the left wing. Beyond, the sward that separated the house from the river was dimly washed in moonlight. Turning the corner, he came upon the French doors to the master bedroom. Immediately inside, beside the bed, was the phone.

Greg slipped over to the nearest door and peered in. Unrelieved dark. But there was no way to know if the intruder had checked the room already or hadn't yet arrived.

And time was passing. Once the police were alerted, there was no telling how long it would take them to respond. After he made the call, Greg would have to get out of the house again, and meet them at the road. So he'd better get going.

He reached for the door handle and turned. Nothing happened. The door didn't budge—and then Greg remembered why. "Jesus!" he muttered. "You idiot!" The door was locked. Days ago, in his bid to make the house seem convincingly deserted, he'd secured every entrance, and the only key he had was for the front door.

His reaction was almost as disconcerting as the discovery itself. Tears came to his eyes, and he had the infantile urge to stamp his foot. A strangled bray of laughter erupted from his throat. He thrust his fist into his mouth, feeling an insane desire to smash the locked door. Then something quite different came snaking up from a place deeper than his rage. *No!* a cold voice commanded. *You will not fall apart now. Pull yourself together.* And, more from surprise than anything else, he did just that.

All right! He had two choices: give up and abandon the place to the bastard he'd so longed to catch, or carry on regardless. There was really only one answer: after all he'd been through, he was damned if he was going to chicken out now.

He circled the house without incident. Ducking as he passed each window, so his silhouette would not be seen against the yard light, he at last reached the front. There was no further sign of the intruder, but he was worried about the crunch of glass if he stepped through the broken window. Then he had an idea: he'd heard somewhere that burglars, after breaking in, often unlocked doors, in case they needed a quick getaway. So, though his key was ready, he first tried the front-door handle. It opened so easily he almost fell in.

Greg recovered and entered, closing the door behind him. The click as the tongue slipped past the striker plate sounded like a hammer in the silence. He froze, quivering, waiting. No movement or sound from any direction.

He enjoyed one small advantage: he knew every inch of the premises. As his eyes adjusted to the gloom, enough of the outside light filtered in to make cautious movement feasible. The bedrooms were down a short hallway to the left, straight ahead was the kitchen, to the right were the dining room and vast living room with its faux native-lodge structure. Greg had caught just one indication of the prowler, minutes ago, in the office. By now he could be anywhere.

The main phone, of which the master bedroom line was an extension, was in the kitchen. It was nearer to his present position but also more exposed. Greg was just weighing his options when his mind was made up for him. Approaching from the living area came footsteps, and a rapidly intensifying halo of light flooded the kitchen.

Adrenalin surged into Greg's gut, setting his heart hammering. Unprepared for the strength of the reaction, he almost tripped as he retreated toward the bedroom. His unconscious grip on the flashlight tightened and turned the switch, producing a brilliant beam of light. Frantically, he fumbled, trying to shield it while switching it off. Mercifully, the light went out, but the after-image on his retina was so strong that he was blinded. He ducked down, trying to avoid the attack that would surely follow.

Nothing. Clearing vision enabled Greg to see that the light in the kitchen was unchanged. And the sounds of searching coming from that direction were also reassuring: somehow, his blunder hadn't been noticed.

The door to the master bedroom was quite close. The intruder's location having been established, Greg's plan of action was clear: go into the bedroom, make his call, then get out immediately through the French doors. But he didn't do that. Reprieve from disaster had made him unexpectedly bold. He decided he wanted to get a glimpse of this soulless bastard who, not satisfied with conning his parents—and being the indirect cause of their deaths—was now trying to rob them again. A quick look, he rationalized, was even necessary, since he would have to be able to identify the person later.

Shifting the flashlight from hand to hand, holding it like a club but now extra-wary of the switch, Greg crept toward the kitchen. He could hear the search there still going on. The guy was thorough, give him that, and seemed to be on the far side of the room. Outside the doorway, Greg dropped to his haunches. Bracing himself against the wall, he peered cautiously around the corner.

The intruder was a dozen feet away, back half turned, fiddling with something on the table. A large flashlight was propped nearby, illuminating the kitchen in stark relief. Greg's first surprise was that the scene looked so mundane. He didn't know what he'd expected—some kind of monster?—but what confronted him was a perfectly ordinary man, about his own size though thicker set, dressed in dark, nondescript clothes, with his hair in a ponytail.

The fellow turned slightly and his activity was revealed: one hand held a mug and the other a bottle. He was pouring Glenfiddich into the mug and raising it to his lips. That was all there was to it: believing himself alone, with all the time in the world to do his business, the guy was taking some R & R with his victim's liquor. That alone would have been annoying, but the fact that what was being casually chugged was his father's Scotch—the one thing that had given Greg himself a little peace—was so infuriating that his present position seemed ridiculous. What was he doing, for God's sake, creeping around his own house like a sissy, when all he had to do was take this guy himself. He'd jump out and, before the bastard knew what was happening, knock him cold, and that would be that.

Greg was so agitated that he couldn't stay crouched down any longer. Stiffly, he stood. Eyes fixed on his opponent, rage becoming resolve, he gritted his jaw and prepared to spring, drawing back the flashlight to strike.

All of this happened in seconds and—as luck would have it—in silence. For just as Greg was poised to leap, the other man finished his drink and from the table casually picked up a gun.

As if struck by some paralyzing ray, Greg froze. The gun glinted in the torchlight, its shape unmistakable, the familiarity with which it was being handled chillingly obvious. It was all Greg could do not to cry out as he backed into the shadows. Safely out of sight, he almost collapsed, fear replacing his former bravado with humiliating swiftness.

But this also brought him to his senses. Even if the man hadn't been armed, had he honestly believed that a surprise attack with a flashlight would subdue him, a character who'd probably been street fighting all his life? By Greg, whose one incident involving fisticuffs had been a failed encounter with a high school bully? What on Earth had he been thinking? He'd come within a hair of a terrible mistake. Miraculously reprieved, he realized he'd better show his appreciation by getting on with what he had to do.

Pulling himself together, keeping a steady eye on the kitchen—from which the man still might emerge any minute—he backed off down the hall. It seemed to take ages to reach the door of the master bedroom, but he was there at last, and no gun-wielding villain had appeared. He felt behind and found the door handle. There was the smallest squeak as it turned, then the door was swinging back. He pushed with his rump, easing into the gap. When he was inside, he quietly closed the door.

He stood in the dark, listening. No sounds came from the other side. He was safe. Against all odds—and despite his alarming stupidity—he was back on track.

But there was no time to waste. It was at last possible to turn on his flashlight, and he did so. The brightness of the beam was dazzling, but his eyes adjusted. There was the big bed and beyond, on a small table on his mother's side—hallelujah—the telephone.

Hurriedly, Greg made his way toward his prize. The phone was a large, bone-coloured dinosaur with an ancient rotary dial. Picking it up bodily—it weighed a ton—Greg was once again struck by just how out of touch with the modern world his parents had been. No wonder they'd been such easy meat for the con man. He placed the phone on the floor on the far side the bed, where the sound of dialing would not be overheard, and shone his flashlight on the venerable instrument. 911: even with a rotary, that wouldn't take long to dial. He peered closer and had just put his finger in the 9 hole when the bedroom light came on.

"Who the hell are you?"

Greg dropped the phone and staggered upright. Standing in the doorway, gun drawn, was the man from the kitchen. He was looking furiously indignant, as if it were Greg who was the interloper.

"I said, who are you?" the man repeated, moving rapidly into the room. "And what are you doin' in my house?"

EIGHTEEN

Greg gaped at the newcomer, unable to utter a word. *His* house? Was the clown kidding? It certainly didn't sound like it. The man's outrage seemed so real that it was hard to believe it was a bluff. Rather than arguing, Greg stood up slowly. The gun didn't seem so frightening up close; it looked almost like a toy, but it could no doubt do plenty of damage. "Hey, listen," he gasped. "Don't point that thing at me. It could go off."

"Yeah, that's right, asshole. It could shoot your tiny balls off. Tryin' to rob me, eh?"

There he was again, acting like he owned the place. Then Greg had an inspiration: maybe, finding someone creeping about in a house he'd been assured was unoccupied, the fellow thought he'd surprised *another* thief, a rival with whom he wasn't about to share. His instinctive, con man response was to pretend to be the owner. "I didn't know you were here," Greg muttered, warily. "Er—sorry!"

"I bet you are," the man snapped. He stepped forward and, looking Greg straight in the eyes, delivered a sharp blow to the centre of his stomach.

Greg's eyes bulged and his frame buckled. After the first explosion of pain, he was convinced that he'd been shot. He staggered back, toppling onto the bed, the wind knocked out of him. Lungs convulsing, he sucked against a wall that seemed to be blocking his throat. He gasped, growing dizzy, and then the dam broke. The sensation of air rushing back was both relief and distress. He coughed violently, dragged in more air, dry-retched, inhaled and coughed a lot more, starting to breathe more regularly as the pain ebbed, and it occurred to him that he'd not been shot after all.

The fellow who'd so cruelly administered this punishment was standing over him. "Lot sorrier now, eh?" he said.

Greg cringed, expecting another attack. Even in his injured state, one thing wasn't hard to grasp: if this villain would attack what he thought was another thief, God knows what he'd do if he found out Greg was the owner—who'd tricked him here to be caught. Stupidly, he'd got himself into a terrible situation. If he wanted to get out of it in one piece, he'd better think fast. "I *am* sorry," he gasped, "for getting in your way, I mean. But you don't own this house. The owners are dead. I know 'cause I live near here. I've been waiting for ages to turn this place over." He sat up and rubbed his stomach. "Just my luck you got here first."

The man gave a short laugh. "Yeah, just your luck. So—if you're a thief too—how'd you get in?"

"I was all set to break in, but then I found the door unlocked. I guess you must have done that. Look, man, I don't do this kinda stuff much, and you look like you're a pro. You've proved you can beat the crap out of me, so I won't get in your way." Greg scrambled to his feet. He wasn't an actor and had no idea how real any of this stuff sounded, but it was the best he could do. "This is your patch, okay? Just let me get out of here and I'll forget I ever saw you."

The man lifted his gun. "You'll forget everything you ever knew if I pop you, creep."

"But why? Look, I didn't mean to move in on your action. And I won't make trouble. I don't even know you, so how could I? Just let me go, then you can look for the money in peace."

Damn! A moronic mistake. As soon as it slipped out, Greg knew it. The man's eyes narrowed. "You know about that?"

"Er . . . what?"

"The money! You said look for the *money*!"

"Well—you know—the guy who lived here was some kind of famous artist. There's always been a rumour that he had a whole lot of money stashed. I guess you heard that too, eh? So I'll let you get on with it. Good luck, man."

He started to edge toward the door. Before he took two steps, the man grabbed his arm. The grip was viciously strong. Greg winced, expecting another blow. He was dragged bodily over to the big standing lamp that was the room's main illumination. The man thrust the gun in his pocket—a good sign?—but then used his freed hand to take hold of Greg's other arm, shoving him roughly into a nearby chair. He peered down into Greg's face for a long time. "Well, fuck me!" he breathed at last.

"What?" Greg said, struggling to rise. "What's the matter?"

"Shut up." The man snapped. "One more word and I really will shoot your ass."

He stepped back and, never taking his eyes off Greg, removed something from his pocket. With one hand, he caught Greg's chin, forcing his face into the lamplight; with the other, he examined the thing from his pocket. Screwing his eyes sideways, Greg could just glimpse what it was: his own driver's licence.

"Well, fuck me," the man repeated. "I thought you looked familiar."

Greg's stomach, barely recovered from the blow, grew sick and hollow. He struggled for something to say, knowing his expression must be saying it all. It had never occurred to him that, having stolen his ID, the man might recognize him. Now the truth was out. How could this have happened? All he'd wanted was a little payback for the wrongs done to his family and himself; all he'd needed was for someone to be accountable. Instead, he'd made a complete mess of the whole thing. Rather than justice, he was looking at the likelihood of his own death.

"You're *Lothian*." The man's voice cut through Greg's morbid thoughts. "The loser whose ID I snagged. What'n hell were you doin' sneakin' round your own house?"

Frenzied words began tumbling from Greg's mouth. "I wasn't sneaking around." He indicated the French doors. "I'd only just got home—late from a party—came in the back way—I was looking around for the light and you burst in. When I saw the gun and then you said this was *your* house, I—well, I thought you must be crazy."

"No kidding." The man's expression said exactly who he thought was crazy. "So you thought you'd just go ahead and pretend to be a burglar?"

"I thought if you thought I was—you know—someone like *you*, maybe you wouldn't hurt me."

"Yeah?" The man grinned nastily. "Or maybe you thought you'd distract me long enough to call the freakin' cops, eh?"

"No," Greg said. But he realized that at least the man didn't know he'd been lured here for exactly that purpose. If that much could be kept hidden, perhaps all was not lost. So he grinned sheepishly. "Well, maybe. But you can't blame me for that. Too late now, anyway."

"You got that right!"

"So there's nothing to stop you getting on with it. You don't need to—*use* that gun. You could just tie me up or something, take what you want and get out."

The man sneered. "Quite the reasonable little guy, aren't we?"

"What do you expect," Greg bleated. "You just attacked me."

"Yeah, yeah!" the man said. "Don't shit yourself. Before I do anything, I reckon you better do something for me."

"What?"

"Show me where the safe is."

Greg's heart plummeted. "Safe?"

"Yeah, the damn safe. And don't try to tell me there isn't one."

"Why—why would you think there is?"

The man laughed. "Oh, yeah. You probably don't know about the letter."

"Letter?" Greg whispered.

"Jesus, you *are* a lousy loser. Haven't you wondered what's happened to your stupid mail lately? I been nickin' it. Your fool sister wrote you this letter, eh? Layin' out the whole situation here. Talked about a safe and a whole pile of cash—don't tell me you don't know about that—in some place called a *studio*. I don't know where that is, so now you can show me." He stuffed Greg's driver's licence away and took out his gun. "Let's go!"

Reluctantly, Greg arose. His ruse had worked all too well. What to do now? Admitting there was no safe and no money would be to reveal his trick, as good as saying "shoot me." Since he couldn't take his captor to a treasure that didn't exist, all he could think of—pathetically—was to play for time.

"I'm not surprised you couldn't find the studio," Greg muttered. "It's not in here."

"So where the hell is it?"

"I guess I better show you."

The man passed his gun from hand to hand. "Yeah, you better."

They left the bedroom, Greg leading the way. At his captor's insistence, he put on lights as they moved along. Evidently, Greg was to be given no chance to use the dark to play any tricks. They reached the back door, but when he went to open it, the man laid a rough hand on his arm. "Where do you think you're goin'?"

Greg's only idea so far had been that once outside, he'd try to make a break for it into the night. "My father's studio. It's out back. A separate building."

"Yeah? Okay—get movin'."

They went out. But either the man was a mind reader or his vocation made him naturally suspicious, because once they were in the open, his grip on Greg's arm never relaxed. They moved along the back of the house, approaching the breezeway that connected to the studio, hardly more than twenty paces. Greg found himself counting, while a dreadful voice inside him whispered that these steps were likely to be his last. The night was so still that out of the dark—into which he'd hoped to flee—came the soft gurgle of the river. If only he could be there right now, he thought, floating to safety. If only he could be anywhere but here. If only he hadn't turned out to be the very thing that this bastard had called him—a loser . . .

They reached the studio. It was locked, but in this case the key was nearby. Hopelessly, his body feeling as if it was already half dead, Greg opened the door and flicked on the lights. The forest of paintings leaped into existence, mocking the dark moment with their beauty.

"What's all this crap?" the man said.

"My father's paintings—this is the studio."

"So where's the safe?"

"Er—actually, I don't know."

"You shittin' me?"

"No! Dad and I never got along. He never told me where—"

"Can it! I don't believe you."

This was it. The end of the line. In the heat of emotion, the man's grip had loosened. With nothing else to do, Greg said, "Oh, hold on, I just remembered," and pointed dramatically to one side. As his captor turned to look, he twisted around and broke free.

He almost made it. He was just going through the door when a savage kick caught him behind the knees and he went sprawling. Immediately, before he could start to rise, another kick caught him in the rib cage. Next came a veritable explosion on the side of his head. Through a cascade of light and stars, he heard himself shriek, then he was grabbed and hauled to his feet. After that, things got even worse. The man, face twisted with fury, held him with one hand while delivering bone-jarring slaps with the other. "Asshole!" he yelled. "Lying cunt! I've killed better guys for less than this. Now it's gonna be you."

But he didn't do it. Not yet. Instead, after a final excruciating slap, Greg was flung into the middle of the studio, knocking down an easel so that he and the painting it had held ended in a tangle on the floor.

Greg lay immobile, conscious of nothing but his pain. Then the hazy outline of boots moved into his vision, and he had enough sense left to try to squirm away. But this time he was not kicked. "Get up!" the man snarled. "Get up, motherfucker, or I'll waste you right now."

Most of what was left of Greg's mind wished that the monster would get on with it: oblivion would be a welcome release. But the last figment of pride and self-respect, faint but undeniable, wouldn't let him give up. Its prompting was insistent, and he somehow found the energy to stagger to his feet.

He stood, swaying, staring through a bloody haze at the nemesis he'd fatally lured into his life. "Right," the apparition gritted, levelling his weapon. "One last chance, loser. Where's the safe!"

Greg continued to gaze at the menacing figure, noting well the naked ferocity that had been unleashed, and his mind did an amazing somersault. The minority voice that had prompted him to his feet now took full control. It was not reasonable, this voice, but implacable—suicidal—and he didn't care. It was the spokesman for all the bitterness and guilt that had consumed him, since the death of his parents and perhaps a long time before. It was the voice of reaction, but also of a sort of triumph. And when it caused actual words to spill from his mouth, these sounded—at least to Greg—like a chant of victory.

"*You're* the stupid loser!"

The apparition stared. "What?"

"There's no safe, you idiot. No money. As soon as I found my mail was being stolen, I knew who must have conned my parents. So I sent that letter to myself. It was a trick, to lure you here to be caught by the cops. The scammer was caught by a scam. What do you think of that, you *loser?*"

The man's expression was Greg's full reward. Knowing what was surely coming, he began to laugh anyway. And as his adversary's demeanour shifted from astonishment back to fury, and the gun hand began to lift, Greg gave a howl and ran straight at it. This took the other by surprise, and he didn't fire immediately. As the two bodies collided, the gun hit Greg's chest, buckling upward and to the side. A moment later, there was a sound like a small firecracker.

That was all.

This time, however, Greg knew that he had been shot. He'd felt nothing, but he had no doubt that his last moments had come. He collapsed backward, impelled by a sensation of great weight. He hit the floor, and the weight, which he understood must be encroaching death, bore him down into what he was sure must soon be the end . . .

He lay a long time, feeling numb, then compressed—eventually just uncomfortable. He opened his eyes to find that the weight pinning him was a human being. The torso was right on top of him, the head resting on his own.

Horror generated the strength for Greg to heave himself out from under. The intruder rolled onto his back, the little gun still firmly clutched, directly under his chin, where it had been knocked before it fired. There was a small hole under the shelf of his jaw and a larger one in the crown of his head. His eyes, apparently fixed on one of Walter Lothian's more spectacular works, registered almost comical surprise.

NINETEEN

Greg had no memory of leaving the studio, but he found himself in the kitchen, gazing at the bottle of Glenfiddich that the intruder had left on the table. The mug that the man had used was still beside it. Numbly, he swept the tainted vessel aside, hardly aware of it shattering as he reached for the bottle. The liquor hit his throat like a small explosion and he gasped, coughed and almost choked before managing to swallow. As the internal fire ignited, he took a few more gulps to get it going. He slapped the bottle down and stood panting, head hanging, leaning on the table, letting his body decide whether it would use the liquor to counteract the shock or just pass out.

After a while, almost to his disappointment, his head started to clear. The heaviness in his chest—the feeling that the corpse of his late tormentor was still weighing him down—retreated, taking with it the sense of unreality he'd been immersed in. He became aware that the space around him was very bright and very still, and that he was alive. The full realization of the odds against that fact very nearly *did* make him pass out.

Some time later, he made his way to the telephone. After a final swig, he abandoned the bottle and, with a sigh, picked up the receiver. 911: he was finally getting to make that call. He had dialed the first two digits when a bolt of panic hit him. "No!" he croaked, and it was as though an unseen force took hold of his hand, slamming the phone down into its ancient cradle.

"*Christ!*"

Breathing hard, Greg shook his head at the treacherous telephone. He'd thought that righteous anger was sufficient qualification to set this ridiculous trap. Now that it had so horribly misfired, did he really believe the cops would pat him on the back and say, "Good job?" God, he wasn't *that* naive. The conning and subsequent death of his parents would be seen as a huge motive for revenge. And with nothing but a few bruises to back up his claim of self-defense, he'd undoubtedly be charged with murder; luring the guy to the house was certainly premeditated. Despite the shocks he'd had, he was sure he was thinking clearly. Greg grabbed the bottle again, then deliberately set it down and put on a pot of coffee. Now he was aware of pain in every part of his body.

The bathroom mirror revealed a face like a freshly mugged vagrant. Resisting the urge to rip off his clothes and get into the shower, he settled for washing his hands and splashing his face with cold water. Then, after downing some Aspirin and two full cups of coffee, he forced himself to return to the studio.

The thief lay where he'd fallen, eyes staring, gun clutched firmly, decorating the studio floor like some bizarre installation piece amidst Walter Lothian's fine art. Unlike the painter, who in death had seemed uncharacteristically serene, this corpse retained a solid echo of its brutality. Contemplating what the fellow had put him through, aware that the body on the floor might easily have been his own, Greg knew he should feel some satisfaction. Yet, even knowing that if the roles had been reversed, the guy wouldn't have wasted a thought on him, all he felt was a sort of dull pity.

Just who was this man, anyway? Greg had become so used to thinking of him as a faceless villain that his having an identity was disturbing. He would have been happier not to know it, for the body to remain anonymous, but his instinct for self-preservation told him that this was no time to be queasy. He no longer feared this person, and the anger that had consumed him for so long was gone, but before he could decide what he was going to do, he'd better find out who he was dealing with.

Greg's attention focused immediately on the gun. Clutched in the dead hand, it looked ridiculously small, almost like a toy, as Greg had thought earlier. It had sounded like no more than a firecracker, yet had been enough to snatch a man out of the world with neat finality. Fascinated, Greg found himself reaching for the insignificant-looking thing. Inches from the burnished steel, his fingers froze.

"My God—what are you doing?"

Horrified, he jerked his hand away. How many times in movies had one seen that tired old cliché: innocent party comes upon a body and, without thinking, picks up the murder weapon? Yet he'd been about to do that very thing. Unbelievable! Greg knew enough of the world to understand that forensic evidence was everywhere, so the first priority was to avoid leaving any trace of himself on the gun.

But he still needed information. And he had a disturbing recollection: somewhere on the body was his own driver's licence, part of the identity theft that had started this whole nasty business. Obviously it would have to be retrieved. That understanding brought an unpleasant fact that had been begging for attention: if he wasn't going to the police, he would somehow have to get rid of the body himself.

Greg went back to the kitchen and poured more coffee. Only then did he think to look at the time, receiving a shock: though it seemed like half an age since the buzzer had warned of the intruder's arrival, it was now only 4:30 AM. But that was okay. It meant there was still plenty of darkness in which to . . . what? As yet, he had no idea.

Under the kitchen sink he found an old pair of rubber gloves. Donning these, he returned to the studio. His first task was to secure the gun. Greg was surprised at how tenaciously the weapon was clutched in the stiffening fingers. Was this the start of what was called rigor mortis? Surely not enough time had passed for that? Having freed the weapon, he placed it gingerly aside, only then examining the corpse itself.

The fatal head wound had done remarkably little external damage: there was just a small amount of blood at both entrance and exit wounds, meaning, Greg supposed, that the bullet must have caused instant death. The frozen leer, centred on the dully staring eyes, was disconcerting, but Greg realized he must be getting used to it, for after a while it didn't bother him too much. He wouldn't have minded closing those eyes, but even with the gloves on, he couldn't bring himself to do it.

The body was very heavy. Because it was lying partly on its side, the only way Greg could get at all the pockets was to roll it onto its back. As it settled in the new position, there was a sudden, loud expellation of gas. Greg gagged and turned his head away, but there was no repetition. He knelt and began to go through the dead man's clothes.

The stolen driver's licence he found almost at once. Seeing his own face emerge from the alien person was creepy, almost like experiencing a physical violation. As he imagined this character swanning about the world pretending to be *him*, he felt the old anger returning. He resumed searching, but save for a bunch of keys, he found nothing else. Certainly no more ID—meaning that if this clown had ever been caught, he would have been thought to be Greg Lothian. Charming! But he couldn't waste any more time in anger. He had to form a plan for what he was going to do with the body.

Bury it? He dismissed that idea as soon as it arose. Aside from the worry of future discovery, the notion of having this unwelcome guest as a permanent resident—even several feet under—was unthinkable. The only alternative was to cart it away, to be disposed of elsewhere. His car was unsuitable for that task, but there was his parents' minivan. Yes, that would have to do.

This decision led to the next requirement: to get the body wrapped and secured for transport. What he needed was a tarp, and he remembered the one covering the Prius. He had it off in minutes, but hurrying back through the dark, he trod on one of the trailing ropes and almost fell on his face. Pausing to recover, he bundled the tarp more securely, then took some deep breaths to calm himself. The night was very still, the sky pierced by a distant carpet of stars. A breath of breeze came from the woods, loamy and sweet; the only sound was the barely perceptible murmur of the river.

Standing quietly, his arms full of crumpled vinyl, Greg turned his head in the direction of the water. Unbidden came an image of his mother, floating to her lonely end, the act that had set off so much more desperation. The result was now lying dead in the very place where Greg and his mother had had their final chat. Thinking of that, Greg made the final—and once it had occurred, obvious—mental leap: the river, which had been the cause of so much pain, could now perform a service.

He laid out the tarp on the floor and rolled the body onto it. Fortunately, this caused no further gaseous emanations. Once it was positioned, he folded the tarp up from the bottom and in from the sides, gathering the residue at the head. This he tied together with rope, making a secure bundle. Thus confined, the corpse could be dragged with reasonable ease, at least across the smooth studio floor. Outside, the going was tougher, but after he navigated the deck and the path, the grassy slope leading to the water was easier again. He slogged along, the trussed burden bumping behind like an enormous Santa Claus sack. The journey was relatively swift, but, though a faint dawn glow was now showing in the east, it was still too dark to see the actual riverbank. Fearing he might plunge over the edge, and realizing he'd need light to get the body unwrapped for its final journey, he went quickly back for a flashlight. Returning, he discovered that the body was not alone.

A dark shape was crouched nearby. When the light swept across it, there was the reflection of two pale green eyes. Greg yelped as the shape bounded toward him and proceeded to leap and lick. "Hatch! What are you doing out?"

Relief was instantly followed by worry. The presence of Hatch might mean that Lucy Lynley was near, though why she'd be walking her dog at this hour he couldn't imagine. He grabbed the dog's collar, extinguished the light and, trying to stroke the wriggling canine into stillness, listened anxiously. Hearing nothing, he came to the conclusion that the dog was probably alone, having an early morning ramble. "Good dog," Greg croaked, with as much command as he could summon in a whisper. "Go home now, boy. Go home."

But Hatch didn't go. When released, he trotted back to the body, sniffed around it, then returned to Greg, tail wagging, as if to say, "Good job." After that he calmly sat and started to scratch himself. Exasperated, Greg realized that he could now see the dog without benefit of the flashlight. Dawn was brightening.

There was nothing for it but to carry on. Now that greetings were over with, the dog seemed content, and he wasn't equipped to tell tales. The growing light revealed that Greg had been lucky to stop when he did. The bundled corpse was resting less than a yard from the riverbank, which dropped steeply to the stones below. From there, the shore sloped away, meeting the fast-flowing river in a few feet. Once the body was deposited on that narrow strand, there would barely be room to unwrap it.

Giving Hatch the apparently unnecessary command to "stay," he rolled the body sideways and, with a heave, over the edge, scrambling to slow its plunging descent. It landed heavily and went on rolling. Stumbling in pursuit, Greg was barely able to stop at the water's edge.

But he did—just. On his knees on the painful stones, grabbing what seemed like an ankle beneath the vinyl winding sheet, he could feel the corpse pulling away as the current tugged at it. He seriously considered letting go, allowing the river to consume his offering unwrapped. But a big, bright blue bundle would attract attention and probably be noticed far too soon. So, once he had a decent grip, he steadied it and walked into the water up to his knees to roll it back up onto the shingle.

Then came the finale. Reversing the wrapping process, he undid the rope that bound the top, folding back the flaps and exposing the body to the expanding glow of daybreak. Lying on his back, staring at the heavens, the villain at last looked passably serene—or perhaps that was just a trick of the light. One side of the tarp was already in the water, so he just had to slide the corpse sideways, to launch it into the current. How far would it be carried? His mother's body had been caught on a snag several miles down on the Cowichan Band's reserve. Given luck, this one would go much farther, perhaps even out to sea. With that hope in mind, Greg stepped back into the water and began to tug the body out into the current.

Then something startling happened: a black shape came tearing down the bank from above. It was the dog, who until now had been watching the proceedings. As the corpse started to slide away, Hatch raced down and grabbed it with his teeth. Aghast at the apparent attack, Greg realized his error right away: Hatch was merely following his retriever's instinct.

"No, Hatch! No!" Greg splashed around to the dog, grabbing for his collar. "Leave it, boy! Leave it now!"

Surprisingly, the dog did. Lucy had claimed he was well trained, and it was true. Mouth open, tail stiff, Hatch backed off, looking at the man expectantly. Greg held out his palm sternly. "Stay," he commanded, and when it seemed that the animal would obey, he once again bent down to the body. As he adjusted his grip, he saw that Hatch's efforts had made a tear in the pants, ripping a back pocket. Sticking out was something square and white.

Greg reached down and retrieved a damp wad of paper. Holding it closer, he discovered that it was an envelope. Even in the pale light, its familiarity struck him like a blow between the eyes.

It was his own letter, the bait that had drawn the rat to the trap.

Had it been found on the dead man, everyone would know exactly where he had come from. And had it not been for the timely action of Hatch, it would already be on its way down the Cowichan River.

Quivering, Greg pocketed the missive, which had almost given the thug the last laugh. "Thanks, Hatch," he whispered. "Oh, man—I owe you big time."

Hatch wagged his tail.

Before anything else could happen, Greg shoved the body out into the river.

TWENTY

The next hour was a blur of activity, of which Greg later had little memory. Although relief was mixed with exhaustion, he knew he couldn't relax until all traces of the intruder's visit—and his own preparations for it—had been eliminated.

Having managed to get rid of the dog, he stored the tarp that had transported the body in the garage. Next he took the telltale letter, so miraculously recovered, tore it up and flushed the pieces down the toilet. Then he went around the house, checking for anything that the dead man might have left behind. He found a small backpack lying in a corner of the kitchen. It contained a flashlight, a couple of chocolate bars and some tools, but nothing to identify the owner. Nevertheless, he buried it in the woods. Lastly, he dismantled his watching post, and removed any evidence of the early-warning device. He wanted to get rid of all physical reminders of the dreadful night. The mental ones were another matter.

Only when it was all done, and the sun well risen on a bright day, did he allow himself to think of rest. A shambling scarecrow of pain and fatigue, he clawed his clothes off and staggered into the shower. The hot water hit him with a delicious shock. His head cleared—and he remembered the gun.

"Oh, Holy Christ!"

Dripping and stark naked, he stumbled through the house. God, how could he have overlooked the most important thing of all? It was lying in the studio, where he had so carefully removed it from its owner's dead hand. The fact that there was no one to see it didn't matter. What terrified Greg was that he could have forgotten it in the first place, almost as if some part of him had wanted it to be found.

With icy clarity, he recalled exactly where the monstrous little thing was. Throwing open the studio door, he almost screamed when it wasn't there. Fortunately, the shock was only momentary; his mental picture had been turned around, and when he looked in the correct place—there was the gun.

He rushed across the studio, so overwhelmed with relief that only after it had happened did he realize he'd actually done that dumbest of things: staring at the gun clutched in his still-dripping hand, all he could do was groan weakly.

But it was too late and—final surprise of the day—he found he didn't care. So his fingerprints were on stupid thing. Okay, before he disposed of it, he'd just have to wipe them off. Meanwhile, he was wet and freezing. He went inside, finished his shower, dried off and without bothering to put on anything, locked every door in the house and went to bed.

He didn't clean off the gun right away. Instead, he stuck it under his pillow.

He awoke at what he was astonished to discover was twilight, from a heavy and dreamless sleep. He felt thoroughly rested, but when he moved, every single inch of him hurt. Rising painfully, he suddenly remembered the gun, stowed under his pillow like a treasured keepsake. *I must have been crazy last night,* he thought, fishing it out. Stripping the case off the pillow, he used that to wipe the weapon from end to end, then dropped it into the case and wrapped it into a compact bundle. Carrying it with him, he padded to the kitchen. Before anything else, coffee.

His bare foot almost immediately trod on something sharp. There were bits of shattered crockery all over the floor: of course, the mug the intruder had used, which Greg had smashed in revulsion and had not had the energy to clean up later. Stepping around the wreckage, he had a vivid memory of the man taking what would be his last drink—then stopped himself in mid-thought. There would be none of that. Not now. Not ever. He would put the whole incident out of his mind, lock it in some dark corner and throw away the key, and that process had to start right now.

While coffee was brewing, he swept up the mess. He then had another shower, which took away much of the pain, and made breakfast. He still hadn't put on any clothes, which, although a little chilly, felt good, cleansing. His parents had often in earlier years gone about the place nude, something with which Greg had never felt comfortable. Now, for the first time in his life, it didn't seem so strange at all. Out of left field came the thought, *Maybe I'm more like the old man than I knew.*

Though Walter Lothian's orneriness had been responsible for much of what had happened in the last weeks, his guts and feistiness had never been in dispute. If, apart from a shared taste for whisky and a newly discovered pleasure in being naked, Greg could find in himself some of the old man's rugged individuality, that would be no small compensation. When memories arose of this fearful time, bringing with them disgust or, God forbid, more guilt, what he had to do, he realized, was view the whole thing through the prism of his father's confidence and self-assurance. Then he would get over it. This was a startling idea that was also a considerable relief.

But what he needed right now was to take leave of the Cowichan Valley. Pack up and return to Victoria. There he could get back to his sane, sensible and, above all, quiet life, while things settled down, in the world and in his own sadly pummelled heart.

As for the gun, the best place for that was somewhere far away from the scene, preferably at the bottom of the ocean.

TWENTY-ONE

After his strange and fearful existence of late, getting back to work was almost like a vacation. Each day, with its peaceful routine, was such a balm to his battered psyche that in a remarkably short time, he was feeling much like his old self. Not that everything was exactly the same. In the office, people treated him differently, seeming to notice him more, stopping to chat when a passing nod would once have been sufficient. At first Greg put this down to sympathy, his parental loss being common knowledge, but it was more than that. He was puzzled, until George Allrod, who noticed everything, provided a clue.

"Morning, Greg," he said one day. "Glad to see you've come out of your shell." Which, perhaps, said it all. For whatever reasons—the deaths of his parents, the frightening aftermath or the simple fact of having survived—the part of Greg that had always avoided interaction with his peers was no longer dominant. The difference was not glaringly obvious, but people evidently sensed it. Quite simply, he was better liked. Once he'd become used to this, Greg found it enjoyable.

The probate of the will was completed in good time, and Greg resumed going to the house by the river on weekends, getting it ready for sale. He didn't sleep there. That would have been too much. And his hours were spent in brisk activity, studiously avoiding all thoughts of recent history. He replaced the broken window and finished the clearing, cleaning and sorting of everything, including the contents of the studio, which he sent to his father's gallery in Vancouver. A huge exhibition and sale of the late artist's works was envisaged for the near future.

When Greg told his sister the kind of sum this was expected to raise, she was as stunned as he had been. They were aware that their father had once been quite famous, but in later years, his style had fallen out of fashion, hence the many unsold works. But death altered everything: the supply of Lothians now being finite, apparently every collector in the country was interested. The amount predicted from the sale was many times that lost in the scam; a mere portion of it would have provided the best possible treatment for Mary. The bitter irony of that didn't bear thinking about.

On a Tuesday morning, nearly two months after the end of the financial year, the second day of summer, Greg received a phone call at work.

"Mr. Lothian, this is D. S. Tremblay of the Victoria Police. I have some news."

"Oh?"

"It relates to the theft of your ID."

"Really?"

"Do you think you could spare a few minutes to come in to the station?"

Greg's heart had speeded up as soon as the caller identified himself. His mouth was a little dry as he said, "Er . . . sure. When would be a good time?"

They settled on 3:00 PM that afternoon. In the interim, Greg continued his regular routine, but the calm that had begun to settle on his soul was disturbed. News about his ID could only mean that at least some of it had been recovered. Did that mean that the body of the thief had been found and identified? If so, the police would no doubt contact everyone whose property had been discovered in his possession. So this contact was probably just routine. Nonetheless, as Greg waited for the intervening hours to pass, he couldn't help feeling nervous.

He got to the police headquarters on Caledonia Avenue long before the appointed hour and filled in time walking about, so that being early wouldn't make him look too eager. But when he did arrive at Tremblay's office, the red-haired detective's friendly greeting immediately put him at ease.

"Thanks for coming in, Mr. Lothian. Take a seat. I hope you didn't have too much trouble getting away from the office?"

"No, we're not too busy at the moment, thanks."

"Fine, fine!"

They chatted for some moments. Tremblay offered coffee, which Greg declined. He couldn't help noticing several pieces of what appeared to be his ID laid out on the desk. Noting his glance, the detective nodded. "Yes, that's your stuff, all right. Does it seem to be all there?"

What wasn't there, obviously, was the old driver's licence. That he had burned. "I guess so," he said, adding, since not to mention it would seem odd, "oh, except the driver's licence. I don't see that."

Tremblay shrugged. "Can't win 'em all. Lucky to get this lot, I reckon. You do identify these items as yours?"

"Of course. Er—how did you find it? You caught the thief, I gather?"

The sergeant patted his brush cut. "Yes and no. That's what I wanted to talk to you about."

"Oh?"

"Yeah. Hold on." Deliberately, Tremblay rose and closed his office door. As he returned, he indicated a picture on his desk: a woman and two young boys. "My family," he said, as if in answer to a query. "You have family, Mr. Lothian?"

"You mean a wife and children? No."

The sergeant tapped his forehead apologetically. "Oh, yeah—you mentioned that, I believe, when you told me the sad story about your parents."

"You remember that?"

Tremblay gave him a look of mild reproach. "Sure! Just because we couldn't do anything at the time doesn't mean we weren't concerned. Anyway, that's kind of why I called you."

"You have information on who stole from my parents?"

"Not exactly. It's complicated." Tremblay reached for a scratch pad and began to doodle. "The reason I asked you here involves a bit more than the fraud committed on your folks, or the theft of your own ID. You see, Mr. Lothian, my guys and the Mounties are conducting a joint investigation into an organized-crime ring operating in the capital region. Obviously, I can't divulge details, except to tell you that your ID was among a bunch of stolen articles we recovered just recently. To tell the truth, it turned up by accident, when we had the unexpected opportunity to search the premises of one of the gang. And *that* happened because the guy turned up dead."

Greg sat very still. "Oh. But I don't see . . ."

"What this has to do with you? Nothing directly. I wouldn't be telling you, except for an odd coincidence."

"What's that?"

"The guy I mentioned was found floating near the mouth of the Cowichan River. You know that river, right?"

"Of course. I grew up there. My parents' house is on the river and that, as I told you, was where my mother . . ."

"Yeah, sure! Of course, you know it all too well, eh? Sorry to have to bring it up, but—well—here's where the coincidence comes in."

Greg strove not to show his growing apprehension. "What kind of coincidence?"

"You see, this dead guy in the river—shot in the head, I guess it can't hurt to tell you that—was found in a place where he couldn't in fact have been dumped. He must have floated down from upstream.

We had no idea where he'd been put in until we got an unexpected break. The Duncan RCMP received a complaint about a car that had been abandoned. When they ran the plates, they found it was stolen. So they took some prints, just in case, and what do you know, they were on file. The thief was none other than our dead perp from the river. So, in finding the car, we knew the general area of where he'd probably got himself wasted. Now—here's where we get to the coincidence—do you know where that car was parked?"

Not trusting himself to speak, Greg just shook his head.

"Can you believe it, on Riverbottom Road—not a hundred yards from your folks' front gate."

"No kidding!"

"Of course, we didn't know the significance right away. It was only later, when we started to go though the guy's stuff and found your ID, that I remembered your story and the Cowichan River connection. So, being a naturally curious guy, I looked up your folks' address and, bingo, it was almost exactly where the guy's car was. Now *that's* a coincidence, wouldn't you say?"

Greg nodded numbly. "Incredible."

"I mean, our guy leaves his car near where someone must have topped him. And that place is connected to one of his victims: yourself. So you see, I have to ask: do you have any information at all that could make this any less of a coincidence than it seems?"

Ever since the revelation about the car, Greg's mind had been churning. How could he have been so stupid? Christ, he had even seen the dead man's keys while searching him. But not until this moment had he given thought to the now painfully obvious question: how had he got himself there? Now, he mustn't let that mistake sink him entirely. The best thing, he decided, was to stick as close to the truth as possible. Taking a deep breath, he said, "Perhaps this guy . . . by the way, does he have a name?"

"Eric Molinara. No harm you knowing that, I guess."

"Perhaps this Molinara went there with the idea of robbing my parents' house."

The sergeant's eyebrows lifted. "*Was* it robbed?"

"No. Otherwise I'd have reported it. What you may not know is that my dad is—was—a pretty famous artist. Because of that, and the way my mum passed so quickly after he did, there was a lot about it in the papers. Maybe this Molinara guy read it, figured the old man was rich, and that the house would be empty and worth robbing."

"And was it?"

"I told you, no."

"I mean, worth robbing?"

Greg gave what he hoped was a realistic chuckle. "Goodness, no. My folks were very old-fashioned. They didn't have any of the electronic stuff that I understand thieves usually go for. Not even a TV set. And as I told you, they'd already been scammed out of most of their money. They certainly didn't keep any in the house."

"But you said your dad was famous."

"Yes, so someone might have thought he was worth robbing. But, believe me, Sergeant, if the guy *had* got into the house, all he'd have found was a bunch of paintings my dad couldn't sell."

"Why not?"

"Because his work is out of fashion. In Canada, being famous and being rich can be two very different things. The irony is that now that my dad's dead, his work is quite valuable again. But no ordinary thief could know that, and it wouldn't do him any good anyway."

"I see what you mean. So—you've no idea why Eric Molinara's car was found where it was?"

"None at all."

"Fair enough. And you didn't notice anything strange at any time? Like—say—odd characters hanging about?"

"No. But you need to understand, I was hardly ever there. Even now that I'm clearing the place out for sale, I can only make it on weekends."

The sergeant nodded, opened a desk drawer and took out a photo, which he slid across the desk. "Ever see this guy?"

Greg willed his hand to remain steady as he picked up the photograph. It was a mug shot of his intruder, a few years younger, posed stone-faced for the police camera, but undeniably the man with whom he'd had the fatal meeting. "This is Molinara?"

"Yeah—minus his extra head ventilation. Well?"

"Never laid eyes on him. Sorry."

"You sure?"

Greg risked a dry smile. "Doesn't look like someone you'd easily forget. Yes, I'm sure."

Tremblay shrugged. "That's it, then. It was a long shot, but you have to follow every lead, even if they go nowhere. In my business, we like to say there's no such thing as a coincidence, but that's bullshit. God knows why Molinara got whacked, or who put him in the river, but it clearly had nothing to do with you. Hell, maybe the clown shot himself. That's what the Mounties think, though God alone knows why he'd do it in a river. Probably we'll never know. Anyway, thanks for coming in."

"That's okay. Sorry I couldn't be more help." Trying to hide his relief, Greg stood up. "Is that all, Sergeant?"

"Yeah," Tremblay said. "Oh, there's just one other thing I should tell you."

"Yes?"

"Apart from the usual spiel about getting in touch if you think of anything else, it's this: the guys Molinara ran with are not small time. He probably didn't steal your ID but got it from whoever did. Frankly, turning over private houses wasn't his style—not unless there was something very valuable involved—so I'd be surprised if your place was his real target."

"I see."

"It's possible that something bigger than we suspected may be going on in your area. Mob guys could be involved, bikers, who knows. To me, Molinara's death has the smell of a hit."

"Really!"

"Yeah. So here's what I'm saying. If you *do* get the feeling of something strange, out of the ordinary, up there in the Cowichan Valley, get in touch with me right away. Would you do that?"

"Of course."

"Good. And don't forget what I said—there could be some very dangerous guys, so whatever you do, don't try to be a hero."

"Don't worry," Greg said fervently. "I'm an accountant. Heroes we definitely are not."

Tremblay's laugh was warm. "Good thing. We need you guys to save us from the taxman, eh? Okay, Mr. Lothian, thanks again."

When he reached his car, Greg realized that the smile that had been on his face when he left Tremblay's office was still fixed there. He got in, only then seeing the parking ticket on the windshield. It didn't faze him. In fact, he didn't even bother to retrieve it, but left it flapping in the breeze as he drove off. When, a couple of blocks later, it flew away, he was still smiling.

TWENTY-TWO

The Montisarian Gallery on Granville Street in Vancouver was modest in its outside appearance: dark glass and burnished bronze façade, name in discreet gold script, beautifully carved but modestly proportioned entrance. Only the presence of a single, glowingly lit painting by the Group of Seven's Arthur Lismer in the front window indicated to the initiated the exclusive nature of the works displayed and transactions conducted therein.

The interior of the place was larger than might have been expected, with interconnected galleries on several levels, all with pale walls and thick carpets, and room for a considerable number of paintings. For two weeks, the entire space had been used to display the works of Walter Lothian: a prelude to the auction.

Greg had come over from Victoria the evening before the sale and stayed at the aging but historic Sylvia Hotel, on English Bay. Jill—who still had not visited the island since their parents' deaths—made what was for her a conciliatory gesture by arriving early to have breakfast with him at the hotel. Although the meeting was cordial, neither had any illusions as to the real reason they had come together; as joint beneficiaries of a sale which had set up a country-wide buzz in the art world, they were merely looking after their own interests.

Enough time had passed since the terrifying events at the house by the Cowichan River that to Greg they were like a half-remembered dream. Because he had refused to think about that night, steadfastly diverting his mind whenever dark images appeared, and since—save for the meeting with Sergeant Tremblay—nothing more had occurred to remind him of it, the twin emollients of peace and time had performed a small miracle of reconstruction upon his equilibrium. Also, in a mild but unmistakable manner, the experience seemed to have brought him out of himself. What had first emerged as a relaxation in his attitude at work had expanded into convivial exchanges, which made him feel among friends.

Greg's sister had also noticed the change in him. When, at 10:00 AM, they were seating themselves in the already overflowing gallery, preparing for the start of the sale, she said, with a sly smile, "All right, Greg, let me in on it."

"In on what?" Greg asked, confused.

She shook her head. "Oh, come on, don't tell me you don't know what I'm talking about. I've been wondering about it ever since we met this morning."

"*What*, for heaven's sake?"

"Something about you is different. Have you got yourself a girlfriend?"

"Don't be ridiculous!"

In fact, during the last months he had been seeing something of one particular girl: pending the sale of the Lothian property, Lucy Lynley had continued to use the studio. While he readied the place for the market, Greg had found himself spending quite a bit of time in her company, occasionally even repeating the enjoyment of her excellent cooking. But girlfriend? To tell the truth, he had occasionally thought in that direction; she was, after all, a very attractive young woman. But she was fully occupied with her mother and her art, while his life was a world away in Victoria. Anyway, what on Earth would an attractive woman like Lucy possibly see in a dull numbers-wrangler like himself?

"It's not ridiculous," Jill said tartly. "What *is* pathetic is you living alone in that stodgy little apartment in Oak Bay, like a crusty old . . ." She broke off, frowning and grinning at the same time. "Except—maybe you're not quite alone. I never thought of that."

"What are you talking about?"

"Have you discovered you're gay? Is that the difference I feel in you?"

Greg had just begun an indignant, if not unamused, denial when the audience was brought to order by the rap of the auctioneer's gavel. The sale had begun.

From the start, it was like something out of a fantasy. The very first painting, one of Walter's more modest West Coast seascapes, took flight, doubling, tripling, then quadrupling its reserve, heading for orbit so swiftly that the auctioneer made no effort to hide his amazement. Rather than being a flash in the pan, this merely served as a spur for the following sales, and excitement mounted until by mid-morning, it was evident that what was taking place was a Canadian art-world phenomenon.

At 1:00 PM there was a pause for lunch, and Greg and his sister retired to a nearby restaurant, not so much to eat as to catch their breath.

After gulping half of the drink she'd ordered, Jill said, "God, Greg, I can't believe it. Have you any idea how much bloody money was paid for that lot this morning?"

The question was rhetorical, but Greg answered anyway. Producing the envelope on which he'd been noting final sale prices, he made a brisk accountant's calculation, jotted the total at the bottom and passed it across the table. When she saw the figure, his sister very nearly spilled the rest of her drink.

At 2:00 PM the sale resumed, with no reduction in pace or enthusiasm. Greg recognized no one, but evidently there were high flyers from all over the country. Some of the bids were relayed by phone. More knowledgeable folk around him whispered the names of a number of prominent institutions, including the National Gallery of Canada, that were represented.

Greg found himself overwhelmed, not just by the amount of money flowing, but by the fact that all this was happening because of his dad. For this memorable response made one thing very clear: somehow, without anyone realizing it—least of all the artist—Walter Lothian had quietly attained the status of a national icon. That this had become evident only after his death was ironic, but hardly uncommon. What saddened Greg was that the fruits of it had not been available, especially for his mother. The fact that he and his sister were now a good deal richer hardly crossed his mind.

The affair ended just after 4:00 PM with every single piece sold. The final tally, even allowing for the gallery commission, was staggering: over seven hundred thousand dollars.

Although, throughout the day, Greg had spoken only to Jill and, briefly, Jules Montisarian, the plump and very satisfied owner, word of his identity must have got about. As the crowd dispersed, several people approached, mainly with congratulations, but also with enquiries as to whether any more works would become available. The last of these departed, along with Jill, who begged off a proposed dinner; this day, though financially rewarding, seemed to have done little to add to the family feeling.

Alone, Greg was somewhat dazedly heading for the exit when he felt a light touch on his arm. A man had approached unnoticed. He was younger than most of the affluent auction crowd, but well dressed, with a pleasantly disarming expression. "Hey, Mr, Lothian," he said quietly. "Went real good today, eh?"

Greg stared at the newcomer; his tone had been casual, but with an odd implication of intimacy. "Yes," he replied. "Er—very well, I think."

"Yeah." The man produced an envelope. "I reckon it's about time I delivered this!"

"What is it?" Greg said, taking the offering anyway.

"Open it. You'll see." He walked briskly to the door, where he turned back, smiling cheerfully. "Nice to meet you," he said. "At last."

He was gone. Only after several seconds did Greg remember the envelope in his hand. It was brown manila, portrait-size, sealed. Feeling a vague flutter in his stomach, he tore open the flap.

Inside was a single photograph. The lighting was harsh, the angle strange, but the subject unmistakable: himself—crouched over the dead body of Eric Molinara.

On the back was scrawled a brief message. *I'll be in touch.*

TWENTY-THREE

For the week following the auction, Greg's mind turned slowly on a spit of anticipation and dread. After the first shock, his impulse had been to tear the picture delivered by the cheerful stranger into a thousand pieces. But that would have been useless. Anyway, he had to keep it close, poring over it endlessly, searching for some clue to how this evil magic had been accomplished. Of course, he came up empty. But the evidence of what had happened that night by the Cowichan River must surely be in the hands of very unsavoury people. Otherwise, it would have been given to the police.

As the days passed and nothing happened, Greg did his best to carry on the appearance of a normal life, while feeling increasingly agitated. One thing was beyond doubt: whatever did finally happen, it was going to involve a price. But what?

When?

I'll be in touch. Simple words, but with implications that grew ever more ominous the longer Greg waited for the other shoe to drop. Then, at last, it did. One morning, two weeks after the sale, when Greg had settled again into some semblance of calm, the telephone rang. "Mr. Lothian," the receptionist said, "I have a gentleman on the line for you. A Mr. Molinara?"

A chill ran through Greg, followed by a hot flush. Guiltily, he glanced about at his empty office. "Mr. Lothian," the receptionist asked, "are you there?"

"Er—yes," Greg gulped, fighting an urge to slam the phone down and run. "Put him on."

"Hey, Mr. Lothian. About time we got together."

The voice was pleasant, but, as before, with a distasteful nuance of over-familiarity. Considering that only a couple of dozen words had passed between them at their first meeting, it was strange how well Greg remembered it. "Is that really your name?" he managed to say at last. "Molinara? Are you a relative of . . ."

"Our river buddy? No way. Business associate. I just wanted to catch your attention. What did you think of the photo?"

Only one thing was in Greg's mind. The words blurted out unbidden. "What do you want?"

"Straight and to the point," the voice said. "Just like an accountant. Cool! Do you still have it, by the way?"

"The photo? It was ridiculous! I threw it away."

The other man chuckled derisively. "Yeah, I just bet you did. Well, plenty more where that came from. Like, a whole collection, if you want to know."

That sounded so preposterous that Greg began to think that this had to be yet another con. He asked, "Why did you wait so long?"

"To make contact? I needed to see if you were worth wasting time on. The big shot picture sale settled that one, eh? You did real good. After that—I guess I just wanted to see which way you'd jump."

"How would you know?"

"I've been keeping an eye on you."

"I don't believe it."

"Have it your own way. We should get together and talk."

"I've got nothing to talk with you about."

This time the laugh was pained. "Mr. Lothian, we both know

that's bullshit. Almost as stupid as me having to waste my pictures on the cops. Everybody loses then, wouldn't you say?"

After a long pause, Greg said heavily, "Okay, how much?"

"What? Look, we can't talk business on the phone. This call is just to make an appointment."

Greg frowned. "You want to come in to the office?"

"No sir! The appointment is for you with me—at *my* office."

"And where might that be?" After he was told, at some length, Greg said, "You've got to be kidding."

"No way. It's a great place for a meeting. Very public, but people are so busy you could go bare-ass and no one would notice. See you there at 9:00 PM tonight."

Before Greg could get out a word of protest, the line went dead.

The season now being full summer, Greg made the trip over the Malahat Drive to Duncan in evening light. The slopes above the winding road glowed green and gold, but to the west, a massive cloudbank reared, a disturbance building in the mountains. Greg paid little attention to his surroundings, however, so engrossed in his thoughts that he hardly noticed the descent into the valley, the straight run to the village of Mill Bay, and the final fifteen kilometres to Duncan. Though he drove with his habitual care, his mind was preoccupied, replaying the grim events that had led up to this unwelcome journey. By the time of the art sale, he'd begun to think the horror was behind him. Now it was all beginning again. Where it would end he hardly dared speculate.

The Cowichan River at the south end of Duncan was the landmark for his unlikely destination. After crossing the bridge, he turned left, his eyes seized by the raw new structure on the southwest corner of the highway. It was enormous—steel, glass, sheet metal and heavy wooden beams, perched on a storey-high concrete platform that served as both parking garage and flood protection from the nearby river. A large sign on the building, its message repeated endlessly in smaller versions everywhere, read: "CHANCES—Cowichan—Fun is Good." The "office" to which Greg had been summoned was a casino.

The building was almost completely surrounded by a parking lot, well lit, Greg was relieved to see. Evening was approaching, abetted by the fast-gathering storm clouds. He locked the car and, feeling like a conspirator in a cheap movie, made his way through the packed cars toward Chances. Though it was only mid-week, the place was jumping, and the broad steps up to the entrance bore a steady stream of patrons. Greg joined the throng, taking curious note of his companions. There were some natives, but they were in the minority. This was a band operation, but most of the punters—at least tonight—were older white folk, largely women.

At the top of the steps, there was a patio in front of a line of glass doors, which opened into the main building. And what a place it turned out to be. Greg, who'd never been in a casino, whose every instinct was to shun such places, was astounded. As he entered the main hall, ahead and to the right he saw banks of glittering, multicoloured slot machines, winking and flashing, each with its gaudy pictures and rows of rapidly changing numbers, letters or images, with names like *Eastern Princess*, *Wild Eyes* and *My Rich Uncle*. To the left was a row of booths for changing money or buying tickets. Two separate, glass-enclosed bingo halls, packed with intent patrons, took up the rear of the vast interior. Blinking signs, indicating two-, five- or ten-cent play areas or jackpots numbering in the thousands, hovered overhead like electronic wraiths. Lines of glowing stars defined the limits of each magical domain. Farther back, a life-size, eerily real blackjack dealer held court from a TV screen. Added to the visual stimuli was sound: a soft but insidious chorus of bells, whistles, pings and half-heard music: urgent, enticing, an auditory counterpoint to the atmosphere of glamour and promised riches.

To his astonishment, Greg found himself momentarily sucked in. The shrewdly calculated ambiance hit his senses like liquor.

Excitement erupted, whispering of ancient longings, forgotten dreams, wealth beyond imagining. Then he drew a sharp breath in disgust.

"Man," he whispered. "What a goddamn con."

As he recovered, his attention was drawn to the behaviour of the patrons. Though tightly packed, everyone seemed in a separate world, perched like zombies over slot machines or bingo consoles, making rapid movements with buttons, levers and coins, immersed totally in the endless electronic ritual. As the man who'd called him had observed: anything could happen here and no one would notice.

To the rear, he'd been told, was a snack bar. It was there he was supposed to be having his meeting. Drifting through the throng, feeling invisible, Greg came to the place. A number of people were lined up for food, patient enough but only half there, longing to get back to the main activity. Nearby was a raised platform with a railing, chairs and half a dozen tables. Just four people were there: an elderly couple with identical hats, munching identical sandwiches, a muscular native sitting by himself in a corner—and the man he had come to meet.

As soon as their eyes locked, Greg knew he'd been watched for some time. The fellow was grinning knowingly, like an old buddy who'd planned a quaint surprise. This both annoyed Greg and made him freshly tense. He scowled as he climbed onto the platform and approached the table.

When he got there, the man didn't move. He just kept smiling, in the end favouring Greg with a satisfied nod. "Cool!" he said. "Right on time." He didn't rise, but casually proffered his hand across the table. "Hey, Mr. Lothian. My name's Jay."

Greg ignored the invitation, sitting heavily opposite. "Okay, cut the crap," he said. "I didn't come to this pitiful place for a chat. You said you've got other pictures. You better show me, or I'm out of here."

The man who'd called himself Jay stopped smiling. For a moment his eyes were very cold, then he shrugged and produced a cellphone. He flipped it open and pressed buttons, leaning over so Greg could see the screen, but keeping a firm hold on the instrument. "There you go, Mr. Lothian," he said. "Knock yourself out."

The screen was small but very clear. The picture showed Greg and the late Eric Molinara, standing opposite each other in the master bedroom of the house by the river. Seeing it, Greg was forced to a startling realization: from the beginning of his encounter that night, someone else had been present. That could be the only explanation. As soon as the image registered, it changed. Greg and Molinara were now leaving the bedroom. Next came a shot of the two headed outside. Then just inside the studio door. Then struggling together, the distance and angle making it impossible to tell who was the aggressor. Then Molinara splayed out dead on the floor.

"Seen enough, Mr. Lothian?" Jay asked.

Greg wrenched his eyes from the telltale phone. "How the hell did you do it?" he whispered.

Jay grinned and snapped shut the phone. "Want a coffee?" he asked. "You look like you could use some booze, but they don't sell it here."

"Rick Molinara was an asshole," Jay said a few minutes later, as Greg stared at him over untouched coffee. "But I guess I don't have to tell you that, eh, Mr. Lothian?"

Greg nodded vaguely. He wasn't sure what disturbed him most, the existence of the pictures, the mystery of how they'd been taken, or the demeanour of the man sitting opposite in the surreal setting of the casino. To his nervousness and discomfort, it was becoming evident that Jay was more than a little strange: what Greg's father, in the lingo of another era, would have called a "weird cat." The over-friendly exterior was an ill-fitting cloak for something darker, an under-stratum of cruelty and spite that peeked around the corners of his smooth façade. Molinara, the villain Greg had foolishly lured into his life, had been frightening in his naked power and aggression, but

Jay, more subtly, gave off an even stronger feeling of menace. Having been spooked into this meeting, all Greg wanted was to be gone. But since he didn't dare leave yet, it seemed he might as well succumb to curiosity.

"That night," Greg asked. "How come I never saw you?"

Jay giggled, in childlike glee. "Because I didn't want you to, of course. You don't have to be embarrassed. Ol' Rick didn't see me either."

"He didn't know you were nearby?"

"Nah! I came with him, and I was supposed to be keeping watch outside. But I didn't trust the mother. He said he was just checking the place out, but I knew he was going after cash. And when he found it, he was going to cut me out. So I kept an eye on him. Hey, Mr. Lothian, you were real smart. I didn't even know you were in the house until he caught you."

"Why didn't you show yourself then?"

"You kidding? With Rick's temper? I've seen him off guys just 'cause they looked at him funny. No offence, Mr. Lothian, but if he was gonna shoot anyone, I wanted to make sure it was you." He smiled. "Who knew you'd waste him instead?"

"But I didn't . . ." Greg began, but Jay carried on as if he hadn't heard.

"What you did after that was cool, buddy. You may be a wimp accountant, but you acted like a pro. All the time I'd been keeping in the shadows and hiding, taking pictures with my cell. At first I thought, hell, if I got some shots of Rick sticking it to you, I could maybe use them to keep the guy in line. And after you told the mother you'd tricked him and there wasn't any money, I really thought that was it. You were going to buy it. But boy, you turned the tables on that stupid guy."

The truth, Greg painfully recalled, was that in a suicidal rage, he'd rushed Molinara, somehow miraculously causing him to shoot himself. Had Jay, watching from concealment, missed this detail? More likely he was ignoring it, though why was another matter.

For the first time since he'd sat down, Greg became fleetingly aware of his surroundings. The ancient couple had departed, replaced by a woman who was wolfing a hot dog while gazing at the video blackjack dealer. The big native man was still sitting in his corner, seemingly in another world. Jay had been correct in one respect, anyway: as a public venue for privacy, the gaming house was perfect. Greg refocused on his companion and said, "Look, never mind who killed who. With Molinara dead, and knowing there was no money in the house—if you weren't going to show yourself, why didn't you just leave?"

Jay chuckled. "Are you serious? And miss the best part of the show? I was gonna have to walk back to Duncan, anyway, since ol' Rick had the car keys. But I wanted to see what you'd do. If you'd called the cops I'd have faded fast, you bet. But you didn't. And the way you got rid of the body—dude, it was brilliant." Impulsively, he produced his cell again. "Hey, would you like to see the rest of the pictures? The light's not great where you're rolling Rick into the drink, and I had to keep back because of that stupid dog, but you can still get the idea."

Greg shook his head, feeling sick. Since it was obvious where this conversation was going, all he wanted now was for the talkative Jay to get to the point.

"Okay," Jay said philosophically, pocketing the phone. "Anyway, like I said, the truly awesome part was the tarp. 'Course you didn't clean it off afterwards. There's probably DNA on it—I guess you figured who would ever think to look. But to be on the safe side, I hid it away."

The last sentence was slipped in so casually that it was a moment before the shock registered. "Hid it? When?"

Jay feigned surprise. "After you crashed. I thought of doing it when I came back later, but I didn't want to take the risk."

"Risk?"

"Of the cops finding it first."

Greg sighed. "You mean, of you not having it to hold over me. All right, Jay, that's enough. No more chat. How much?"

"Much?"

"Money, damn it! Stop playing around."

In the peculiar cross-currents of light spilling from the surrounding sea of slot machines, Jay's eyes flickered and glowed. "Money?" he said. "Buddy, I don't want your stinking money."

"Then what on Earth *do* you want?"

Jay looked bewildered, convincingly hurt. "Have you been *listening*? I said you were clever, eh? Brilliant. I never saw a guy in such a load of trouble come out so good. You're a survivor, friend. A brain! And you've got that great pad. All hidden away by the river. You could have a super grow op there, a meth lab, anything. Not only that—you've got the cash to finance a major operation."

Greg just stared. "So what are you saying?"

"Mr. Lothian!" Jay replied, shaking his head. "Have I got to spell it out? What I'm *saying* is that we're going to be partners."

TWENTY-FOUR

Greg was out the doors and across the patio before he was aware that he was walking through a near-solid sheet of rain. Unnoticed in the electronic cocoon of the casino, the weather disturbance, threatening earlier, had blossomed into a massive summer storm. Before he was halfway down the steps, Greg was soaked, but he paid no attention. With the dazed aspect of a gambler who'd just lost his last dime, he found his way to his car, got in and just sat, motionless and steaming, oblivious to discomfort and the pounding of the rain, everything but the nightmare of his meeting with Jay.

Some time later, automatic reflexes came into play and he started the car. As he headed out of the lot, the rain still so thick that the car's wipers could barely cope, one practical fact did penetrate: there was no way in this tempest he was going to drive over the Malahat to Victoria. Instead of turning right onto the highway, he went left and crawled through Duncan, climbing the Trunk Road hill and heading west out of town. What would normally have been a twenty-minute drive to the house on Riverbottom Road took longer than the journey to the city on a good day. On the last part, the winding, tree-shrouded road was nearly invisible, due to the water sheeting across the headlights. Following it would have been hopeless had he not known every twist and turn, in a mental map etched from childhood. As it was, at a recently created junction where the old road had been washed away by some previous storm, he almost missed the turn and barely avoided ending up in the river. By the time he arrived at the house, the concentration he needed for survival had carried him past his first shock into a clearer state of mind. Unfortunately, this only emphasized the dire reality of his situation.

Over the months, coming out to the house on weekends, he'd done much of the work to prepare it for sale, finding it therapeutic and a change from his usual sedentary routine. The garden was neat, and most of the small junky stuff removed from the premises, though he had yet to start on the furniture. But the upheaval caused by his original encounter with Jay had left him stunned, unable to think straight, and his efforts had sputtered to a halt. Now, not only was the place not ready, but a dangerous and probably crazy man was planning that it not be sold at all.

In the kitchen, Greg stripped off every stitch of sodden clothing, including a business suit that even a trip to the cleaners might not save, and went to the whisky cupboard. Of the stash of Glenfiddich he'd originally discovered, one full bottle was left, plus about a quarter of another. He poured a glass of neat Scotch and had a couple of solid gulps. Fire erupted in his belly, a welcome antidote to the hard lump of anxiety that had been growing there. He took the glass and the rest of the bottle into the bathroom, got the shower running as hot as he could stand it and went in, taking his drink along. The shower had a little shelf where he could place the glass. Slowly, he turned his body round and round under the steaming jet, pausing at each completed 360 degrees to take a gulp of liquor. By the time he had made ten revolutions, the glass was empty and—suitably cooked inside and out—he was feeling a little less anxious.

Which left just the disgust.

Greg got out of the shower and toweled off. He poured some more Scotch and moved through the house to his sister's old room, where he'd been sleeping and keeping the clothes he used for working around the place. But the garments looked unwelcoming, a physical embodiment of the trap that seemed to be closing in. And though the storm had cooled the air, he was still feeling pickled from his shower. He slipped on an old pair of thong sandals and, naked, drifted back to the kitchen. Decanting the last of the whisky bottle, he opened the kitchen door and stood sipping and staring out at the rain. It was still sluicing down, and now there came the close rumble of thunder, preceded by jagged bursts of lightning, which rent the sky and were reflected in the turbulent river.

Wryly, Greg thought that this ungovernable stew of electricity, wind and water, which was turning the laboriously tidied property into a sopping, branch-strewn mess, was a perfect metaphor for his own situation. Like the storied butterfly that, flapping its wings on one side of the world, causes a tempest on the other, a single decision on his part had led, by inexorable degrees, to disaster. He was a mild guy, a quiet guy, and all he'd ever wanted from life was to be left in peace. But now, because he'd tried to use a little ingenuity to bring justice, he was shackled to the villains he'd desired to punish. Through ill luck—as well as his own hubris and stupidity—he'd put himself into their power. Simple blackmail would have been bad enough, but that at least was finite; when the cow was milked dry, presumably it would have been discarded. But *this* demand, that he use his resources to promote the worst sort of crimes, as an alternative to being charged with murder, was just too dreadful to think about.

A particularly vivid lightning bolt crackled across the river, seeming to head straight in his direction. Instinctively he ducked, smiling grimly as he realized that if the bolt had indeed had him in its sights, he'd already be fried. That got him thinking along another tack: if he were to stand in the open, in the rain, out in the middle of the lawn, when the next lightning struck, his troubles might be over.

He shook his head sadly. Whatever else, an end like that would be just too embarrassingly messy. The idea of his naked carcass lying like a hunk of over-barbecued beef, to be discovered, perhaps by Lucy Lynley, was not to be contemplated.

Anyway, despite everything, he didn't want to kill himself.

He closed the door and fetched the last of the whisky from the cupboard. This time he didn't bother with a glass but took a swig straight from the new bottle. Carrying it absently by the neck, he wandered through the house, putting on lights as he went. He began to envisage the place as it might well be in the near future, crammed with marijuana plants under the harsh glare of grow lights or filled with the stink of some frightful and vastly illegal chemical brew. The idea was so nauseating that he tried to stop the thoughts, but could not. He pictured the kind of people who—if the dreadful Jay had his way—would soon be frequenting this place: criminals, thugs, burly bikers and hollow-eyed dealers, the scum of the Cowichan Valley. Then other scenarios began to unfold, prompted by the fact that, in his tortured wanderings, he'd reached his father's studio.

It was empty of Walter's paintings, but a few unfinished sketches remained, along with several bright oils by Lucy, one still in progress. That got him imagining her reaction upon discovering the shameful thing that had happened to the property of her old neighbours. Naked as he was, he grew hot all over, just picturing her face. But if things worked out as planned, dared he even let her find out? His new associates no doubt had ways of dealing with people they imagined to be a threat. What had Jay said of Rick Molinara? That he offed people "just 'cause they looked at him funny."

The thought of Lucy, cold and dead, floating down the river with her throat cut, was momentarily so vivid that Greg physically recoiled, taking an extra-large drink. Some of the stuff went down the wrong way, causing him to cough violently and almost drop the whisky. This made him pay attention to the bottle, and he realized that a third of it was empty. He paused, shaking his head. He didn't feel drunk. In fact, the way the evil imaginings were crowding in, he wished he were drunker. Yet, since arriving at the house, he must have consumed half a bottle of single malt Scotch.

He shrugged and went to drink again, then stopped. Yet another image had arisen, a memory this time: the night—what seemed like years ago—when he'd discovered his dad's stash and taken a shot to settle his nerves. Compared to his usual occasional glass of wine, that first drink had produced a buzz that was pure bliss. Since then, the whisky had helped him through many an anxious moment. He'd even started buying it himself, with the assumption that when this frightening time was over, he'd return to his old ways. The trouble was, he liked it. Needed it. And tonight proved that he could now go through a great deal without much benefit at all.

He was becoming addicted.

At that realization, the last and worst image exploded: himself, an end-of-the-line alcoholic, staggering about the property while the odious commerce raged all around, cut off from the straight world, scorned by the hoods he'd brought into his own, waiting only for some brute to show enough mercy to put him out of his misery.

That last picture galvanized him. If only to banish it, he dashed out of the studio, running as fast as the awkward sandals would allow. He didn't stop till he was in the open, in the full force of the driving rain. He threw his head back and screamed. When a lightning flash glowed red on his closed eyelids, he didn't move a muscle, thinking—half hoping—that this might be his last moment. But it wasn't. Instead of a jolt of killing current, all he felt was the pounding of water and the buffeting of wind against his skin.

He opened his eyes, perversely relieved and disgusted. Then he was running again, sloshing his way down the grassy slope toward the river. Another lightning flash showed him the edge, and the water boiling by. A single thought was in his head: to get rid of the whisky bottle, to toss the foul thing into the torrent so that some small part of this nightmare might be over. This—*this at least*—would stop!

At the river's edge, another flash revealed that the water was even higher than he had thought. This seemed prophetic, cleansing. Swaying inches from where the flood was racing by, Greg drew back his arm and flung the bottle wildly. He didn't see it go, since at that moment the dark was total, but seconds later, despite the howl of the elements, he was sure he heard a splash.

"Yeah!" he yelled to the sky, and all the evil legions who were coming to ruin his life. "How's *that*, you rotten bastards?"

For a glorious moment, the feeling of triumph was so intense that Greg bellowed a huge laugh and clapped his hands together. That caused his balance to shift just enough that his left sandal lost its grip. Teetering, he instinctively threw his weight onto the other foot, which held for a heart-stopping second and catastrophically let go. Then, in a natural outcome of physics, gravity and alcohol, Greg's body flew out from under him with such speed that he was hardly aware when the water on his skin ceased to be rain and became the deadly embrace of the river.

TWENTY-FIVE

After a desperate time of sinking, writhing confusion, there was a sensation of rising, then of released pressure on his head. Unable to wait to make sure he'd broken the surface, he gasped, rewarded by a rush of mostly air down his tortured gullet. He coughed and sucked in again, paddling wildly to keep above water. The current was moving fast, pulling him along in what, for all that his eyes could register, might have been an underground storm drain. This river, which he'd enjoyed during many a carefree summer, had gulped him down, flushing him away in a most unseasonable passion.

Despite the turmoil, he had stark images of other bodies taken by the torrent: his mother, who had chosen it, and Molinara, who had not. Through no will of his own, it seemed Greg might soon be joining them—and maybe that was only fitting.

The darkness was broken as a great sheet of lightning seared the sky, and Greg finally got a glimpse of his position. He was in the middle of the river with twenty feet of swirling hell on either side. He turned his body to face the direction of the current, and immediately something came from behind and bashed him on the head. It was a huge, uprooted tree. Had it not been travelling only slightly faster than himself, it would have killed him. He was thrust beneath the surface, gulping in liquid before he knew what was happening. The resulting distress in his chest compounded the pain caused by the tree.

Consciousness began to recede. In slow motion, he twisted around, somehow managing to break the surface, choking and flailing as other roots and branches attempted to pull him down again. Instinct made him grab a handhold, but only after he'd spluttered himself into some semblance of relief did he realize he was firmly attached to the tree, riding with it down the river.

Was this good or bad? If the trunk rode up on rocks with him underneath, crushing or drowning would finish him quickly. But the risk was worth it, if the tree bore him to where he could reach the bank. If only he could *see* the bank. But never mind: now that he had hold of this solid thing, he wasn't going to let go.

Several more flickers of lightning, in quick succession, enabled Greg to see where he was more accurately. The ordeal must have been briefer than it seemed, because he hadn't been carried very far. Peering back, over the swell of the bank and through the driving rain, he could just make out the glow from his own place. He strained upward in the water, waiting for the next flash to show him how far he was from shore. The lightning came, but at the same time as the very thing Greg had feared: with a crack and a shudder, the tree hit something large and unyielding, irresistible force striking immovable object. As the tree slewed and jerked, the branch that Greg held whipped skyward, snatching him bodily from the water. Rather than being trapped, he was flung right over the trunk and plunged into the dark depths on the far side.

He had time to suck in a breath before he went under, but now he was being rolled and tumbled, aware only of his shock and fast-fading strength. He tried to right himself with feeble arm strokes, but that got him nowhere, and soon he was in desperate need of oxygen. Need expanded to discomfort, then to agony in his mid-regions. He had to use every ounce of will to prevent his lungs from going into spasm and forcing him to fatally suck in water. He was almost out of time. Defeat and doom were the price demanded by this monster river. The sooner he capitulated, the better. But he couldn't. Not just yet. In a last frantic effort to delay the inevitable, his legs flexed and thrust down.

His feet brushed over stones.

For a moment the news didn't register. Nevertheless, primitive pathways conveyed vital data to his nervous system. Legs and arms reached out, scrambling for the land that he now knew was there. His first actual thought was a surge of joy as his feet struck bottom, then pistoned him to the surface. His head broke out and air screamed down his throat. He flopped back, but got another full breath before going under. Then he surfaced again, leaping and slipping, plunging and jumping, sideways to the current, up a steady incline that was leading to shore. The water was at his thighs, his knees, his calves: at ankle depth he slipped and fell flat, cracking knees and elbows on the stones, but hardly feeling the impact. He lay flat, head to one side, gurgling, panting, sucking precious breaths of life.

At last, prompted by a vague warning that if he didn't move, he might pass out, he crawled through the shallows. Stones became gravel, water gave way to a rain-drenched strand. He moved up until gravel was replaced by the softest pillow, which, with fuzzy wonder, he recognized as grass.

That was his last thought.

A baby was crying. The sound was right in his ear. He realized with irritation that the infant was sucking and drooling on it. Someone ought to feed the brat, he thought, or at least remove it, so he could get back to sleep. But that didn't happen. And after a time it seemed that the wailing noise was more like that of an animal. A dog. But he didn't own a dog. If he had, he certainly wouldn't have allowed it on the bed . . .

"Hatch. What is it? What have you *found?*"

He became aware of a voice, calling from some distance. It seemed vaguely familiar. At last, the woman must be coming for her baby—her dog—whatever . . .

"Where are you, boy? Oh, there—oh *no*!"

The voice was right above him—almost a scream—too loud. And there was bright light wavering on his face. Damn! Couldn't she just take her dog and leave him in peace? Without opening his eyes, he weakly tried to wave her off.

"*Greg!* Thank God—you're alive! How did . . . ? What are you doing . . . ? Hatch, back off. Oh, dear—hold on!"

Hands were on him, rolling him uncomfortably on the bed. And the voice, which he realized must be his mother, kept chattering senseless questions while her hands were on him, slapping, stroking, then, when he began to shiver violently, pulling up the covers . . .

He opened his eyes.

The figure crouched above him, outlined by some sort of light, was definitely a woman. But not his mother. Of course, his mother was . . . "*Lucy?*"

"Greg, you're conscious. Thank Heaven! What were you . . . ? Never mind. Gotta get you up. Can you move? Come on, you're going to die of exposure! Up—up—we can do it . . ."

The assault on his body was relentless. As he somehow became vertical and started to stagger along, propped and half carried, propelled by the sturdy legs beside him, he had no idea of what all this might mean. He just knew that, despite the confusion and jolting disarray, he felt surprisingly peaceful. Right foot, left foot, over and over, waver and recover, on and on and on . . .

Then, bright light and more commands. "Look out—watch—*up now*." Hazy vision showed steps, which his feet—for some reason, bare—were being urged to climb. Then they were moving again, over a smooth surface, through air that seemed as mild and welcoming as a warm bath. A little later there was another voice, female too, but older—that surely *must* be his mother—expressing shock and concern from a long way off.

At last, the voices faded. His legs, which, despite the help, seemed now to be straining through molasses, were stopped by something firm. A gentle force from behind made the top half of him keep going. He toppled forward, coming to rest in the most welcoming place he'd known since leaving his mother's womb.

Curled fetus-like, he slept.

TWENTY-SIX

He awoke in a haze of gold. At first he thought he was still dreaming, then came the slow understanding that he was conscious, lying on his back, with what felt like sunlight shining on his face. He'd dozed off while taking a rest from working in the garden; that must be it. He couldn't recall exactly what he'd been doing, but he felt so deliciously comfortable that for a while, he couldn't be bothered opening his eyes to find out.

Then doubt came seeping through a crack in his contentment: this didn't feel like the outside. He opened his eyes, squinting in the bright light. Sun was shining through uncurtained windows, cheerily illuminating the place where he lay: not a garden, but a bed. He sat up, moving his head out of the light so he could properly see his surroundings. The bed was in a strange room: chintz, floral wallpaper, pretty knick-knacks, painted furniture: a fairy-tale scene, which Greg regarded with astonishment.

Then his attention centred on an anomaly: a neatly folded stack of adult-looking clothes on one of the chairs. This caused him to become aware of his own body, which he discovered was naked beneath the bedclothes. Surprise deepened into confusion and embarrassment. What in hell . . . ?

Then it all came back.

The process of remembering didn't have the mercy of gentleness.

It was like a trap door opening on an abyss. Revealed in brutal detail were the events that had led to his waking up—by some miracle—in this improbable place. He closed his eyes, as if *that* would shut out the flood of the sickening saga, and groaned.

There came a tapping on the door, low but insistent. "Hello?" Lucy's voice called. "Are you awake?"

Greg turned his groan into a weak affirmative, and Lucy opened the door. Seeing him sitting up, she smiled and entered briskly.

"Good morning."

"Er—hello."

"Well, don't *you* look better! The poor drowned rat has turned into a regular Adonis."

The words perplexed him; well, the "drowned rat" bit was obvious enough, but "Adonis"? Then he got it, blushed and, in a gesture he instantly regretted, pulled the sheet up to his chin. "Oh, man, I'm sorry," he croaked. "I didn't mean to embarrass you."

She smiled and sat on the bed. "Don't be ridiculous. What would have really embarrassed me is if I'd found you dead. Anyway—you gave Mum the best thrill she's had in years."

"Your mother . . . ?" That detail, at the near-unconscious end of his ordeal, had eluded him. "Oh, shit! I'm so sorry . . ."

"Don't be silly. This isn't the nineteenth century. All we care about is that you're okay."

Greg relaxed a little. "Yeah, thanks," he began. Then something else arose, a fierce necessity that had to be attended to right now, and he said, "Lucy, listen, I know I owe you all kinds of explanations . . ."

"If you think so . . ."

"I do! And I will. But there's *one* thing I must tell you right now."

"That you didn't jump into the river on purpose?"

He stared. "How did you know?"

Lucy smiled palely. "Because I know you. Your mother might have needed to end things that way, but you never would. Look, after we'd got you in bed, I went over to your place to see if I could find out what had happened. I found it deserted, doors open, lights blazing, an empty whisky bottle in the kitchen and your wet clothes in a heap. Okay, it even looked like maybe you'd got wasted and decided to take the easy way. But Greg, I just knew there had to be more to it than that."

"Why?"

Lucy smiled in exasperation. "Because you're so damn straight."

"Oh."

"No, I don't mean dull, or goody-goody. I mean—well—pig-headed. Easy ways out just aren't you. If they were, you'd have let your father run your life and become a bad artist instead of a good accountant. That's all I know. And hey, I was right, wasn't I?" She squeezed his hand and rose. "These clothes are some of my dad's. When you feel like getting up, I'll make breakfast."

"Thanks. Now that you mention it, I'm ravenous."

"Okay, good. And then . . ."

"Then?"

"Maybe you'll finally tell me what's going on."

Later, relaxed and fed, dressed in Lucy's father's clothes, which fit him quite well, seated in the kitchen, Greg unburdened himself of the entire story. To his relief, Lucy's mother wasn't present; telling the truth to Lucy was hard enough. Starting with what she already knew—what she, indeed, had revealed to *him*—the "account inspector" fraud, he told her about his own troubles: the identity theft, the diversion of his mail, which, by providing the criminals with information, had led to his parents' deaths, his terrible guilt, which in turn had brought inspiration, and the trick that had turned out so fatally. He left nothing out. When he reached the part about Jay, the outcome seemed so obvious that Greg was embarrassed not to have foreseen it.

"I just had the meeting last night in that awful casino place in

Duncan," he concluded wearily. "I thought Jay would want money, but it's worse."

Lucy, who had listened transfixed, shook her head. "What could be worse than blackmail?"

"He's decided to make me his partner."

Lucy frowned. "*Partner?*"

"Using the property—and my money—to make and sell drugs."

"And if you refuse?"

"He's got the evidence to get me convicted of murder."

"But you didn't kill anyone!"

"Who's going to believe that?"

"Does he have the gun, too?"

"No. At least I got rid of that."

"How?"

"Threw it off the Johnson Street Bridge in Victoria."

"Well, certainly no one will ever find it there." Lucy laughed suddenly.

"What?"

"I was just thinking—you may not be a crook, but you seem to know how to cover your tracks."

"Don't joke. What I am is a damn fool."

"I'm not joking, actually. And you're not a fool. You tried to do a good deed. In your own way, to right a terrible wrong. And you might have pulled it off. If your parents knew what you tried to do, they'd be proud."

"Yeah? Dad would think I'm a moron."

"You're wrong. Walter may have been bad tempered, but one thing he did admire was guts. He had more than most people himself. That's what helped him keep going after his work stopped being fashionable. It also made him pretty impossible, I'll agree, but he was a fanatic about—as he saw it—doing the right thing. And that, incidentally, is why you're so much alike."

Greg's jaw dropped. "You're kidding!"

"Come on, Greg, do you think just because he was into art and you like figures that you're so very different? That's just what you *do*. What you *are* is like mirror images. He all bluster, you all ice. But you're equally stubborn and, frankly, with the same sort of blindness about each other. Yes, I know I'm talking as if Walter were still alive, but you know what I mean. And if he *were* here now, he'd see what he'd missed in you: someone amazingly like himself, with a whole heap of integrity and courage."

Lucy stopped, looking awkward.

"Wow!" Greg breathed.

"Sorry," Lucy said. "I didn't mean to embarrass you. But it *is* what I believe."

Greg smiled. "The truth as you see it, eh? You've certainly never been one to hold back on that. Probably that's why Dad thought you were so great. Anyway, I'm not embarrassed. With anyone else, maybe. Not you. I just hope I can live up to what you think of me. Especially, right now, the 'courage' bit."

"Lucy, dear?"

The voice was that of Shirl Lynley, calling from farther off in the house. "Oh, goodness—Mum!" Lucy said, rising. "This time of day I usually help her dress." She headed out of the kitchen, turning at the door. "Greg, she was very worried about you. Could you come and just pop your head in? She'll be so happy to see you're okay."

Greg nodded and followed Lucy through the house. When they arrived at Shirl's room, he did as requested, stopping at the door and standing where the old lady could see him. She was sitting, well propped with pillows, looking frail but alert as her gaze met his own. She smiled with such evident affection and relief that any mortification Greg might have felt at having paraded before her in the altogether slipped away. "Morning, Mrs. Lynley," he said from the doorway. "How are you today?"

The woman's smile took on a tinge on amusement. "As well as can be expected, dear. More importantly—how are *you*?"

"I'm okay. Much better—thanks to both of you."

Her smile deepened. "Not forgetting Hatch, of course. He's the one who found you, I'm told."

"I'll make sure to thank him too."

After the laugh, there was a pause. The three looked at each other, a host of things unsaid. Greg presumed that Lucy would tell her mother the whole story. Then Shirl turned to her daughter and said, "Dear, I don't think I want to get up yet, after all. Just give my shot and help me get comfortable. And maybe bring me a little more tea."

Lucy began preparations for the first task. As Greg was about to leave, Shirl re-engaged him with her steady gaze. "You see, I have a wonderful daughter, Greg."

Lucy made dismissive sounds. Greg said, "I certainly do see that."

Lucy plumped pillows so energetically that her mother restrained her. With a quiet smile, she said, "Nothing is quite so humbling as having our children do for us what we used to do for them. But I don't know what I would do without Lucy." She planted a kiss on Lucy's hand and gently pushed her daughter away. "Forget the tea, dear. I'll have it later. And I don't need the insulin yet. Off you go now. I'm sure you two have lots more to talk about."

They left her there and returned to the kitchen. Their talk certainly wasn't finished, but somehow, without having come to a conscious decision, Greg knew what he had to do.

TWENTY-SEVEN

As he approached Victoria Police Headquarters, a study in modern steel and glass that still managed to look like a cop shop, Greg paused, thinking, *What if they never let me back out again*? He grimaced, then shrugged philosophically. Whatever happened as a consequence of this action, it had to be better than the alternative. He'd considered hiring a lawyer to accompany him to the meeting. That might have been prudent—possibly he was crazy not to—but he hadn't, largely because it would make him feel so guilty. If that was his attitude, he knew he'd probably act like it, which could be fatal. Considering all that had happened, his only hope was that the police would believe his story. *Good luck on that, buddy*, he thought wryly. Then, squelching the last-minute jitters, he went in.

Sergeant Tremblay was at his desk, poring over a file and scratching his red buzz cut with a pencil when Greg appeared. Since he had made an appointment, the policeman showed no surprise. Something in Greg's manner must have alerted him, however, because, having waved his visitor to a chair, he rose and closed the door as he had before. He wasted no time with formalities, but put his elbows on his desk, leaned forward and said simply, "Okay, Mr. Lothian, how can I help you?"

Greg knew that there was no quick or easy way to do this. So, much as he had with Lucy, he started at the beginning and told the whole story.

The sergeant didn't comment, question or otherwise interrupt. He just listened, occasionally giving the tiniest of nods. But as the narrative progressed, his expression, though remaining scrupulously neutral, took on a distinctly glazed undertone. This intensified until, when Greg was describing his meeting with Jay at the casino, his face was like a pale mask.

The only detail Greg omitted was his late-night plunge into the Cowichan River. Since this was merely the result of mischance and whisky, and added nothing to the salient facts, he felt he could at least spare himself that humiliation. He also left out the fact that he'd already unburdened himself to his neighbour; indeed, he made no reference to Lucy at all, figuring that she had enough on her plate without being brought into this. He ended by relating Jay's threats and outrageous plans, letting that stand as the reason for his belated decision to come clean.

When he was done, the silence was so complete that Greg could hear the traffic going by on Caledonia Avenue and a burst of laughter from the office next door. Sergeant Tremblay was no longer looking at him directly. Face still mask-like, he seemed to be examining a spot somewhere above Greg's head. He impulsively squeezed his eyes shut and rose, as if propelled by invisible springs. Three strides took him to the window, where he stared studiously down at the street. For several minutes he remained thus, while Greg watched, not daring to move or say a word. At last, like a statue on a slowly revolving plinth, the sergeant turned. His face was still blank, but now, instead of pale, it was nearly as red as his hair.

Then Greg almost fell backward as Tremblay launched himself across the room and in less than a second was towering over his chair. His hand flashed out and Greg winced, expecting a blow. But, rather than striking, the sergeant's strong fingers grabbed Greg's jacket and hauled him to his feet.

Oh, man, this is it! Greg thought. *He's going to tell me I'm under arrest for murder. Damn, I should have brought that lawyer, after all.*

But that was not how it went. Having glowered at him, eyeball to eyeball, for several long moments, Tremblay released his grip, allowing Greg to sink back into his chair. At last the sergeant spoke, voice barely more than a whisper. "Who else knows about this?"

Greg gawked dazedly. "Come again?"

"Are you suddenly deaf?" Tremblay snarled. "I said, who else *knows?*"

"Nobody! I've told no one."

Other than Lucy, of course.

"Okay, okay!" the sergeant breathed. "All right, then." He rubbed his hands together briskly, as if warming them, stared at his fingertips and then at his visitor, while Greg thought, *What's happening? If he's going to arrest me, why doesn't he get on with it?*

"Do you know the Starlight Café?" Tremblay said.

"What?" Then, as the cop seemed about to explode again, Greg continued hurriedly, "Sorry, it's just . . . yes, of course I do."

"Good. Now listen." Sergeant Tremblay backed off and hovered, hands on hips, still getting himself under control. "Pull yourself together, pay attention, and don't make me repeat myself again. In one minute you're going to leave this office. You will look perfectly relaxed and normal, as if nothing important has been happening. You will not—*repeat, not*—speak to a soul, and you will leave as quickly and quietly as you can. From here you'll go straight to the Starlight Café, where you'll get a table in the quietest damn corner you can find and wait for me. I may get there in minutes, or it could be a whole lot longer. Whatever it takes, you will wait, and again—apart from your server—speak to no one. If there's any part of this you don't understand, tell me now. Otherwise, just nod."

Numbly, Greg nodded.

"Oh, yeah," Tremblay continued, in a different tone. "There *is* one alternative I should mention. If you've got problems with any of this, you can always come with me down to the cells right now. Is that by any chance what you'd prefer?"

Silently, Greg shook his head.

"Okay, Mr. Lothian. So what say you get the hell out of here?"

TWENTY-EIGHT

The Starlight Café was a Victoria institution. As venerable, if not exactly as old, as the Empress Hotel, it had the advantage of being off the obvious tourist routes. Instead of being a tarted-up parody of itself, like so many venues in pursuit of the tourist dollar, the Starlight had remained true to its genteel past. Serving fine tea, passable coffee and splendid, creamy treats, the café had been able to maintain its perch in the fast-food world due to an influential and fiercely loyal clientele, plus long-established proprietors not totally obsessed with the bottom line. The Starlight was an eatery out of yesteryear, well-mannered and quiet, its only eccentricity being the name; ironically, the place had never been open after the time respectable folk head home for supper—5:00 PM in the afternoon.

Greg entered and, as instructed, found himself a secluded table. It took several minutes for service to find him there, but he was familiar enough with the place to be unsurprised. When help did arrive, in the form of a kind-eyed waitress with white hair and a broad Yorkshire accent who called him "love," he ordered coffee, then sat back in his dim corner, trying vainly to relax.

He had no notion about the reason for this assignation. Curiosity fought with apprehension, but eventually he gave up trying to figure it out, thankful simply to be sitting in a marginally comfortable chair rather than a cell. He waited an hour, had two coffee refills, went once to the toilet, decided he'd better ask for the lunch menu, was just checking his watch for the umpteenth time when—almost like an illusionist's trick—there was Tremblay approaching the table. Greg had noticed the sergeant's powerful build earlier, not realizing that he was capable of moving with such stealth. With barely a pause, the officer dropped into the opposite chair and leaned across the table. His face was neither flushed nor wax-pale now, but the look he fixed on Greg was so intense that he fancied he could almost feel heat.

"We are not here!" Tremblay said.

Knowing better than to say anything, Greg made a vaguely quizzical head movement and waited.

"Neither cops nor perps hang out in this place," the sergeant continued, "so there's not likely to be anyone to know different. You *are* clear on that, eh?"

Greg nodded vigorously. The waitress appeared and Tremblay ordered a pot of tea. Since it was approaching noon, the café was starting to fill, but their isolated corner remained quiet. Not until the tea appeared, Greg's coffee had been refilled yet again, and they were alone, did the one-way conversation resume.

"All right," the sergeant said, "first things first. *Yes*, I believe you're a gibbering idiot. *No*, I don't believe you're a murderer."

Greg felt the knot in his stomach begin to relax. "Thank you."

"Just thank your lucky stars that I'm not a by-the-book guy, like some cops I know," the sergeant snapped. "And if *that* observation—let alone the rest of what I'm going to tell you—ever gets beyond these walls, I'll not only see you're charged with murder, I'll even cook up the evidence to make it stick. That clear?"

Greg's knot began to return. "Very."

"Okay!" With surprising delicacy, which blended oddly with his still-simmering anger, Tremblay poured milk into his cup and added tea. Having taken a sip, his eyes once more bored into Greg's. "Were you ever in the service?"

Presuming, after a moment of uncertainty, that the sergeant meant the military, Greg shook his head.

"Well, I was—before I became a cop. In the army. Even saw some fighting, in Bosnia and West Africa. Military operations have commanders and planning guys who look like they know what they're doing. But mostly they don't. Have you any idea what actual warfare is, when it comes down to it? Shambles! Chaos! Once the lead starts to fly, no one has time to think about damn all, except how to stay in one piece. Even when battles are won, it's often as not by accident. And you want some news? Police work isn't much different. Oh, we've got lots of good guys who do their best and sometimes they get it right. But it's a goddamn war out there: a *world* war, that's bust its way even into our little one-horse town. And, what with drugs and guns and kiddy porn and terrorist mania, it's getting tougher by the minute. Like the military, we cops like to pretend we've got it covered, but really it's a mess. We don't have enough of anything—men, money, resources—and every day's a running battle just to keep up. Add to that the time we waste trying to cope with idiots like you, and it falls apart."

Greg flushed. Whatever he'd expected, it was not to be accused of being the last straw in the breakdown of society. His expression must have shown this to comical effect, for Tremblay unexpectedly gave a snort of laughter.

"Oh, hell," he snapped. "It's a hobby horse, okay? You made me mad and set me mouthing off. Now listen. I've been checking, and there's nothing I could find that would make me disbelieve your story. That doesn't mean that you haven't been bloody stupid. It also doesn't mean that some sort of charges may not be laid eventually. It all depends on how it turns out."

"Turns *out*?"

"Well, you don't imagine this is over, do you?"

"I don't know."

"Whatever your motives, as a civilian you've been acting inexcusably. Let's take that as read. And now, as a cop, I'm doing the same thing. If anyone knew we were talking like this, I'd not only be out of a job, but probably up on charges myself. Obstruction of justice, for a start."

"But surely you don't intend to . . ."

"Obstruct justice? No. My plan is to help the warty bitch all I can—though that's not how my bosses would see it. But never mind about that now. Let's talk about that perp you wasted."

"Molinara? But I told you, I didn't . . ."

"Just kidding. The important thing right now is that the guy's dead. This wouldn't be considered evidence, but do you know the thing that convinces *me* you didn't do it? The guy was such a smart and evil fucker, he'd never have given you the chance to off him: he *had* to have somehow done it himself. And that's one hell of an irony."

"How come?"

"Because there are at least three killings—two the Mounties have been working on and another one here in Victoria—that we've been trying to pin on *him.* Molinara was a real bad dude. Mob connections, a whole string of felonies going way back, kidnapping, arson and attempted murder. We wouldn't expect him to be doing small-time stuff like B and E, except you made the bait so tempting. A safe full of cash? Very smart."

"I only wanted to . . ."

"Yeah, yeah, no need to explain. You were just too damn clever for your own good." He chuckled. "Though screwing up by dropping your phone in a coffee cup has got to be classic: I must put out a warning memo to my guys about that. Seriously, the fellow you dumped in the chuck was a very bad man and you've done the world a service, but don't expect me to ever admit I said that. But I've gotta tell you right now—the other one is just as bad."

"Jay?"

"Yeah. Just to make sure we're talking about the same guy . . ." Tremblay produced a photo, which he slid across the table. "Is that your friend from the casino?"

Greg examined the picture. It had apparently been taken from a distance, but the bland, oddly smiling face of the fellow was clear enough. "That's him. But look, he's no friend . . ."

The sergeant cut him off with a shrug. "Stop being so uptight. We're agreed that you're a good guy, okay? But right now, teasing your ass is the only thing stopping me from kicking it. So shut up and listen. This Jay is a little hood, originally from the Duncan area, called Jules Riley. A few years ago he moved east and ended up pimping for the mob in Ontario. But he got on the outs with one of the heavies and someone tried to top him. Shot him in the head, but he survived. I don't know if that scrambled his brains, but afterwards it seems like he was a regular oddball. Got to be such a pain that half the hoods in TO were after him. But the guy's one cagey little jerk. Good at sneaking around and turning up where he's not expected. So, the next thing that happens, the guy who shot him, plus a buddy and a woman they were bunking with, are all found in a house up in Markham, very dead. There's evidence that Jay was responsible; he vanishes. Nothing's heard of him for months, then he turns up here . . ."

Tremblay broke off and waved to their elderly waitress. Without preamble, he ordered food—"any kind of sandwich"—which Greg, with little enthusiasm, seconded. Not till it arrived, quite swiftly, did the story resume.

"The reason I know so much about this creep," the sergeant said through a mouthful of pale bread, "is because we've got a guy in Vice who used to be with the Toronto cops. He recognized that picture I showed you. It's from a surveillance we were conducting on some other hoods, one being the late Mr. Molinara. He was from Toronto originally, and we figure they met there. Anyway, Jay was ID'd and we kept coming across him while we were keeping tabs on Molinara.

We'd have pulled him in, but we didn't want to jeopardize a big bust we've been helping the Mounties set up: that's the police business I couldn't tell you about before. But after Molinara was killed, Jay dropped out of sight again."

"Seems like he was keeping busy following me," Greg said.

"Exactly. With his buddy deep-sixed, Jay was probably wondering what to do next—till you gave him the perfect idea."

Greg reddened again. Tremblay wasn't going to let him forget his folly any time soon. But it was also clear that this clandestine meeting had not been set up just for the purpose of embarrassing him. The sergeant wanted something, and Greg had the unpleasant feeling that he was soon going to find out what it was. Thinking that he might as well get it over with, he said, "What do you want me to do?"

Tremblay looked shocked: no, closer inspection showed that the expression was an intentional parody. "*I* don't want you to do anything. How could I? Didn't I say at the beginning that we are not here?"

Greg sighed. "Right. But we're not sitting at this table for a reason. Could you cut the explanations and tell me what it is?"

The sergeant allowed a faint smile. "All right, here's how it stands. We and the Mounties are involved in a big undercover operation—drugs, cross-border people-smuggling, the works—and we're just about to pull the plug. Molinara was one of the bunch we were hoping to nab. But maybe Jay is too. We're not sure. This thing he wants to get into with you could be an independent operation, or he may be hoping to use it to get an in with his new mob. Whatever, we don't dare move on him until our big bust has gone down."

"When will that be?"

"Very soon. Any day now, so I've got to make sure that no one gets spooked. Here we come to the part where you, as a civilian, get to know what I, as a cop, can't officially tell you to do. If this purely hypothetical line of action should later occur to you as your own idea—and also some kind of payback for all the trouble you've caused—then I'm not going to be around to dissuade you."

Greg smiled grimly. "I get the idea. Describe this hypothetical line of action."

"It's simple enough. What you do is play along with Jay."

"That's it?"

"Yeah. I don't know how long you'll have to stall the guy. With any luck, just a few days. But during that time you'll have to keep him happy. Convince him that you're scared and you'll do anything he wants. To keep it looking real, you may even have to start the cash flow. But I hope it'll be all over before he's cleaned you out completely."

"Thanks a lot," Greg said sourly.

Tremblay shrugged. "You're the accountant. You'll think of ways to hold things up. Anyway, the most important thing is to take things easy. You've shown you've got a good imagination. Use it to keep your friend Jay calm and yourself out of trouble—while, of course, keeping me informed."

"Oh, man," Greg breathed. "That's a job for a professional."

"Precisely," the sergeant agreed blandly. "That's why I would never ask you to do it. But, if you decide to go ahead anyway—to take the law into your own hands, much as you did in the case of Mr. Molinara—then you may end up doing a whole lot of people, not the least yourself, a very big favour."

Greg breathed deeply, stared at his half-eaten sandwich, then gazed into the pale eyes that had never left his face. "Wow," he said at last. "For a cop, you're some piece of work."

Tremblay sucked air softly through his teeth. "For an accountant, so are you. Well?"

Greg sighed. Finally, he said, "There is one thing I'm going to need, I guess."

"Which is?"

"Another cellphone."

TWENTY-NINE

"How long would you need this time?" George Allrod asked.

Uncomfortably, Greg regarded his boss, whose patience he felt must surely have been tested to the limit. "Hopefully only a few days. But it's sort of—open-ended."

"Mmm . . . You've already had a lot of time off, and the client list is growing, due in no small part to your own efforts, I might add."

"Thanks. I'll put in extra hours when I get back."

"I just wish you could tell me what's the trouble. No more—er—family losses, I hope?"

"No, George, nothing like that. It's just—personal business."

The senior partner's kindly face creased in worry. "Greg—forgive me for bringing this up again, but since your parents' passing, you've changed, come out of yourself, which, of course, is good. But you also seem quite distracted. I hope this doesn't mean you're dissatisfied with your place here."

"Goodness, no," Greg said hastily. "If my job was the only thing I had to worry about, I'd be the happiest guy in the world. Actually, what you noticed is sort of connected with why I need to get away. But when I come back, everything'll be back to normal. I promise."

Allrod smiled. "Good to hear. There's also the partnership we talked about. I trust you're still thinking about that?"

Becoming a partner of the criminal, Jay, was the only thing he could think about right now. But he said, "Definitely. I just hope this won't put me out of the running."

"Certainly not. You're one of our best people, as I've often said. Okay, Greg, do what you have to do and return as soon as you can. We'll manage somehow. Off with you—and good luck."

Considering what he was facing, he was going to need all the luck he could get. Still, his boss's good-natured acquiescence did make him feel a little better. The office represented his real life, and just to know that it would carry on smoothly was a comfort.

He returned home and spent the rest of the day cleaning his apartment, making ready for what might be a prolonged absence. He also collected all the documents he would need to convince Jay that he was going along with his plan, mostly those that would seem to facilitate the withdrawal of large amounts of cash. He didn't mean to do this, of course; he intended to stall as long as possible. The proceeds from the art sale were what Jay had his eye on. As executor of his father's will, Greg had full access to that, but he didn't intend to lose *any* money, if it could be helped. He'd have to invent some legal problems to buy time. As Tremblay had said, use his imagination. Since he had no idea how soon Jay would demand cash, or, indeed, how long this charade would go on before the police were ready to intervene, all he could do was hope like hell he wasn't bankrupted before the axe fell.

One vital detail he had not taken care of, however, was Lucy. After his meeting with Sergeant Tremblay, he'd phoned, if only to let her know that he wasn't in jail. He wasn't sure how she'd react to what he was doing, or if he should even tell her. Mainly, he wanted to make sure that, for her own safety, she kept well away from the property. Calls to her house only got the answering machine. Shirl, Greg knew, was unable to come to the phone, and Lucy, what with looking after her mother, her painting and all the rest, was pretty busy. But since she neither answered the phone nor returned his calls during the day, he decided that as soon as he got out to the river, he'd better pay her a visit. He wouldn't have to tell her everything, just enough to make sure she stayed well out of harm's way.

A call he *did* receive, however, later that afternoon, was one that he'd been expecting. "Hey, old buddy, how's it hangin'?" Jay said, in the overly familiar tone Greg was beginning to loathe. "Just calling to make sure you're heading out to the house."

"Yes. When will you be arriving? Tomorrow?"

"Nah! We need to talk tonight. Make plans."

"Well, all right. But give me time to make the place ready."

"For what?"

"Well, you know, for a guest. Where are you now?"

"Out and about. Some stuff I have to do before I move in with you. Hey, that'll be a kick, eh, pal?"

"What's that?"

"You and me—two buds—hangin' and bangin' and runnin' a real cool game. Duncan is really screamin' for a proper drugs source. Lot more fun than that shitty casino. We'll be rollin' in green before you know it."

"Yes—sure."

"But my suppliers don't work on credit. We're gonna need a pile of working capital. You've got that taken care of, eh?"

"I'm working on it."

"Sweet. Well, just wanted to check in. See you later. Take care driving over that old Malahat. Ciao."

The phone went dead. Greg put down the receiver distastefully. He was reminded of another communication that had come in on this same little-used landline, the message about the phony cheque that had alerted him to the theft of his ID. However, morbid meditations on that subject were curtailed by another reminder: his new cellphone, on which he'd keep in touch with Sergeant Tremblay and—very soon, he hoped—receive news that his ordeal was over, was still charging on the kitchen counter, the only thing not packed for his journey.

He added it, grabbed his bag and started out. At the door, he paused. His apartment, which had earlier taken on an unfriendly feeling, now looked so familiar and safe that he could have wept.

"Yeah," he muttered. "*Now* you tell me."

He closed the door quietly and headed down to the car.

Near the top of the pass, Greg pulled in at the Malahat Mountain Inn, a restaurant overlooking a fiord-like gouge of ocean called Finlayson Arm, on the east side of the island. He didn't stop there often. Though the food was excellent and the view spectacular, the place was expensive and usually too crowded for his taste. He hadn't intended to eat dinner but he was hungry, and the urge to delay his arrival at the house was strong. Since he didn't mind being seated inside, forgoing the attractions of the panoramic dining deck, there was no wait for a table. He repressed the urge for a large whisky and ordered a glass of wine, followed by a well-spiced pasta. He didn't much enjoy the meal, but he did end up feeling more relaxed. And when, in late evening light, he arrived on Riverbottom Road, his thoughts, if not rosy, were at least upbeat. Things had gone badly, but he now had a chance to redeem himself. In a very real way, his actions would help with the rounding up of a whole bunch of criminals. Playing a tricky game with Jay for a few days was surely well worth that.

When he arrived at his gate, he found it closed. Did that mean that Jay hadn't arrived? No, more likely he'd shut it behind him, not wishing to advertise his presence. But when Greg drove into the courtyard, he found no other vehicle. He felt relief, knowing this to be pointless. His "partner" would be there soon enough and then the act would begin. That was going to take all his cunning and ingenuity, and the sooner he got used to the idea the better.

Anyway, the fact that no vehicle was evident and the house was dark didn't necessarily mean that Jay hadn't arrived. He seemed to enjoy creeping around unseen. Maybe he was doing that now, waiting to give Greg a surprise on his own turf, thereby emphasizing his power and control. With that in mind, when Greg unlocked the front door and entered, he called out loudly and confidently, as if he knew perfectly well that Jay was present.

There was no answer to his greeting.

He kept moving through the house, checking first the kitchen, then the living room, finally down the hall to his sister's old bedroom, where he deposited his bag. By that time he was pretty sure that he was alone.

What to do now? Since all he could do was wait for the inevitable arrival, which must surely be soon, he decided he'd better try to rehearse in his mind the cowed, obedient fellow that he had to pretend to be.

He went into the kitchen, his eyes moving automatically to the drinks cupboard, saddened but relieved that the whisky stash was gone. A belt of Scotch would have felt good, no doubt. But remembering where it had got him last time, and knowing he was going to need every bit of focus he could muster in the days ahead, he was happy to settle on coffee. He had just started fixing a pot when the telephone rang.

Startled, Greg wiped his hands and hurried to the phone. "Hello?"

"Greg! Oh, thank God, at last!"

Such was his surprise that it took Greg a moment to register that it was Lucy. "Lucy—hey! I've been trying to get hold of . . ."

"Greg," Lucy cut in. "I can't talk. I'm sorry, I just had to . . ."

There was a fumbling sound, snatching away Lucy's words in mid-sentence. This was followed by a click, a pause—then something else entirely.

"Hello, Mr. Lothian," the voice of Jay said quietly. "What took you so long?"

Greg heard himself gasp and tried to recover. "How—what's going on?"

"A party! That's what!" Jay replied.

"*Party*? Where?"

"Your girlfriend's place, of course. And, Mr. Lothian—you're the guest of honour."

THIRTY

When he left the house, Greg broke into a run, though there was barely enough light remaining to show the path. It would have been quicker to go the long way around by car, but he'd been ordered to come on foot; there was to be no chance of anyone witnessing his arrival at Lucy's. His other instruction had been more ominous: he was not to contact anyone in the meantime. Failure to obey would result in unspecified harm to the women. Greg had already made too many near-fatal errors in his career as a crime buster to even consider ignoring that one.

By the time he reached the end of the Lothian property, he could hardly see. Here the path left the riverbank, entering the woods that enclosed the open area in which the Lynley house stood. It was at this point that Hatch often intercepted him, but no dog appeared tonight.

As he stumbled along, cursing the fact that he'd been too flustered to bring a flashlight, the only thing thicker than the surrounding gloom was his own confusion. How could this have happened? How could Jay even know about Lucy, let alone turn up at her place? Now, it seemed, the women were to be used as some kind of leverage against him. That could only mean that Jay no longer believed he had enough control to get what he wanted. But how had such a change come about? Greg was still wrestling with that question when he emerged from the woods.

Relief that he could now see his way was countered by his rising concern. There were lights on in the house, but the shades were drawn. The porch lamp was also on, outlining Lucy's car in the driveway, as well as a dark-coloured van that Greg did not recognize. Not until he skirted around these, arriving in the pebbled forecourt, did he get an uninterrupted view of the steps and the front door.

Sprawled on the stoop, in a pool of blood, was the body of an animal. It was Hatch. The dog's eyes were wide and empty. The gore in which he lay came from his neck; his head was almost completely severed. Under the merciless glow of the porch light, the scene vibrated with surreal clarity.

"*Oh, Jesus!*"

Greg turned away, feeling his gorge rise. But a worse sensation overtook the nausea: cold fear. He stared numbly at the house, fronted by its dreadful talisman. As if on cue, the door opened and a figure appeared, a man so large that his shiny black hair flirted with the lintel. Though the angle of light made his face a silhouette, the features were clearly native. Jay had a sense of familiarity as the giant stepped forward, kicked the dead dog aside and made a curt beckoning gesture.

Greg didn't move. Fear had coalesced into an agonizing knot in his solar plexus. But he knew he had to go in. As the newcomer beckoned again, this time with greater emphasis, Greg started to walk. Up the front steps he went, trying to avoid the remains of the dog, past the huge native, who regarded him impassively, and into the hall. Everything here was normal except for one detail: across the polished wood floor there was a trail of blood. Blood was also spattered on the native's pants and heavy boots. Greg was trying to ignore this, steeling himself to keep moving, when a voice was raised farther off in the house.

"That you, Mr. Lothian?"

It was Jay, sounding cheerful, almost jocular. The contrast of the tone to what he'd just witnessed was so weird that Greg felt a fresh chill. But he kept on walking, doing his best to avoid the blood, all the way down the hall.

The first thing he registered upon entering the living room was the figure of Shirl Lynley. She was lying on the sofa, in a familiar position, but though her eyes were closed, she looked far from comfortable. Her head was resting on the arm of the sofa at awkward angle, and she was very still. For an instant, Greg thought she was dead.

Then his focus shifted to take in the room's other occupants. Lucy was behind the sofa, frozen in the act of reaching for her mother, as if she wanted to touch her but did not dare. Jay was off to the left, watching Greg with a small smile.

In his hand was a blood-covered knife.

"What the hell's going . . . ?" Greg began, but he was interrupted by a small explosion of sound.

"All right, you bastard," Lucy snapped, swinging on Jay. "Greg's *here!* Now, for God's sake, let me get my mother back to bed and give her her insulin."

Shirl winced and her eyes opened, which Greg noted with relief. After a pause, Jay shrugged and nodded. Lucy came around the couch and, simultaneously, the big native moved in from the door. They reached the older woman together. But Lucy stepped into the man's path, glaring ferociously. "Don't touch her," she cried. "Don't you dare lay a hand on my mother again."

The features of the big man didn't appear capable of much expression, but he did look questioningly at Jay, who shrugged again. "Whatever."

The native stepped away. Lucy leaned down to her mother. "All right, Mum," she said, her tone painfully tender, "it's okay. We can get you back to bed now." She put her mother's feet on the floor, then, stooping and taking most of the weight, was able to get the frail old woman upright. Greg anxiously watched the two shuffle forward. Reaching him, they paused, Shirl swaying while Lucy fought to keep her steady. Lucy's head turned, her angry eyes meeting Greg's. "This is your fault," she whispered fiercely.

"I'm sorry. I don't know how . . ."

"He killed poor Hatch. Had his goon drag Mum out of bed, then he cut the poor dog's throat in front of us. To show he meant business, he said. And the next one . . ." She gave a swift glance of awful significance at her mother.

"No!"

"*Yes!* He even *said* so. But you're here now. So it's got to be over. I don't know what this crazy man wants. But whatever it is—do it."

"Believe me, I will," Greg spluttered.

"And for God's sake—*get them out of here*."

After the women had departed for the bedroom, Greg turned back to find Jay regarding him calmly. The young man had seated himself in an armchair. From that angle, Greg could see a detail he had not previously noticed: a small but deep indentation at the hairline forward of Jay's left temple. Shot in the head, Sergeant Tremblay had said, thereafter becoming a "regular oddball." Lucy had called him crazy, which right now seemed more appropriate. Jay was looking at him with his odd smile. "Wow, Mr. Lothian," he chuckled. "I can see I was dead right with this call."

"What are you talking about?"

"You're sweet on that bitch, admit it."

Rage made Greg throw away all caution. "You damn animal!" he snapped. "How dare you break in here! How dare you threaten these people! Whatever the hell you think you want from me, just leave the women alone."

In reaction to this outburst, Jay just stared. Then his hand, which had been hanging out of sight, rose up, still holding the bloody knife. This he plunged into the arm of the chair with such force that the blade vanished almost to the hilt. Using the handle as a lever, he sprang to his feet. "It's your fault, you double-crossing prick," he spat.

"Even the bitch could see that. Whatever I'm doing, it's all because of *you*!"

Greg was so appalled, he could barely whisper. "What are you talking about?"

"You and that fat-assed cop!"

Greg gaped. He aware of blood rising in his face. Far too late, he said, "What cop?"

Jay hissed in almost comic exasperation, and began working his knife free from the chair. "Are you completely stupid? Didn't those pictures I took of you and Molinara tell you *anything*? I follow people, you asshole. That's what I *do*. I've been checking on you ever since that first night. Didn't you think of that?"

In fact, Greg had thought of it. Not seriously enough, apparently. Glumly, he waited, as Jay got the knife free and wiped the blade on the chair.

"I've got a big investment here," he continued angrily. "Did you really believe I'd rely on a few pictures to keep you in line? Do you think I'm that dumb? Whatever else, there's still seven hundred grand at stake here. You seemed like pretty much of a wimp to me, but hey, I thought, maybe I'm wrong about that, eh? Maybe I'd better have a Plan B. So I keep following you, waiting and watching. I see you've got this girlfriend next door, with her crip mommy, and the three of you are real thick. I also follow you in town. And what do you know? Pretty soon you're heading for the Victoria fuzzhole. Then you and this fraud-squad dickhead, who I've seen around before, meet up in an old-lady hangout, where you think you won't be seen together. What does that tell me? Dickhead cop and asshole partner are planning to set me up."

Jay had been pacing. Now, passing the large native who had been immobile near the door, he indicated the man with his knife. "Oh yeah, this is Trev. You may remember him from the casino? We went to school together. He's pretty pissed with his buds in the band right now. Looking for money to get out of here. If you want to find out what he's prepared to do to make that happen, try double-crossing me again. Trev didn't kill that fleabag mongrel, but he was real happy to hold your girlfriend while I did. And he'll do it again—if I have to teach anyone else around here a lesson. Are we on the same page now?"

Greg didn't answer. What he'd been listening to sounded like a scene from a bad movie. But it was real. The man truly *was* mad. And this final situation was his own fault. Were it not so frightening, it would have been ironic.

Jay was shaking his head. "Now I've found out I'm being double-crossed, I say to myself, 'Okay, Jay, don't waste time being pissed. On to Plan B.' So that's what I do—and here we are."

Although he'd rather not have known, the question had to be asked. "What's this Plan B?"

Jay shrugged. "You're looking at it, buddy. This is where I'm going to hang out from now on. Well hidden, with the two bitches for insurance. Meanwhile, you're going to phone your cop buddy, tell him there's no sign of me but you'll keep him posted. Then you get me that seven hundred grand. All of it."

"What if I can't get it?"

Jay swung around to the big native, Trev, giving him a brief nod. Without expression, Trev left the room, returning presently with Lucy. Just inside the door, he stopped, his prisoner writhing in his grip. When she began to cry out, Trev put one huge hand over her mouth. There they remained, Lucy's eyes wild, Trev's face patiently blank.

"Listen carefully," Jay said. "Back east, I'm wanted for some stuff that could pretty much get me prison for life, okay? So I've got nothing to lose. Killing that mutt was just to get your attention. *This* is what you need to know."

He strode over to Lucy, held securely by Trev, and raised his knife, holding it an inch from the woman's throat. "If, for *any* reason, I don't get that money," he said quietly. "Or if I get the smallest smell of a cop . . ."

Jay made a slashing movement with his knife, so fast and close that, for a horrified instant, Greg was certain the worst had happened. But no mark appeared, no grisly spurt of crimson erupted; though tense and quivering, the pale throat was unharmed.

Greg's own gullet had contracted and his heart pounded. Slowly, he lifted his gaze from Lucy's mercifully intact neck to her terror-filled eyes, finally making himself look at Jay.

"Well, Mr. Lothian?" Jay said.

"I understand," Greg's replied, voice barely a whisper. "I'm sorry. I've been stupid—but no more. No one will ever know you're here. And that money, I promise—*I promise—I'LL GET IT.*"

THIRTY-ONE

"Lucy, I'm just so sorry," Greg said. "Are you all right?"

Lucy, who was looking flushed and dishevelled but little the worse for her ordeal, nodded grimly. "I'll live. It's Mum I'm worried about."

"Nothing more will happen to either of you. I promise."

"How can you say that?"

"Because—you heard me—I'm going to give him what he wants. This is just a ransom situation now. Once Jay's got the cash, all he'll want to do is get out of here."

"And you won't tell the police?"

"Of course not. I won't do anything that would run the risk of harming you."

"It's an awful lot of money. Can you really get it?"

"Yes."

"How long will it take?"

"I'm not sure. The funds are in the account. But it's a small branch, so I doubt that they'd have that much cash on hand. A day or two at the most. Will your mother be all right for that long?"

They were in Lucy's room, where, with Trev standing guard, they had been permitted a short time together. "I have all her meds, and there's plenty of food in the house. Mum will be okay." Lucy indicated their stone-faced jailor. "As long as that brute doesn't start manhandling her again."

"He won't. I'm sure Jay just wanted to scare us. He made his point."

Thinking of Hatch, Greg hoped he was right. But he couldn't afford to let himself dwell on that. Only action would suffice now: getting the money as fast as possible, and being especially careful that Jay had no other reason to be provoked. He once again apologized to Lucy, and asked her to say the same thing to her mother. As he prepared to leave, Lucy gave him a fast, fierce hug. The contact caused an unexpected glow, but it didn't last.

The back door of his house was hanging open, just as he'd left it. Exhausted, mind in a turmoil, he found himself pacing up and down the living room. There was nothing to be done until the morning, he knew, but the idea of waiting until then was torture. His watch showed that it was only 9:30 PM, which he scarcely believed; it felt like days since he'd arrived.

Sergeant Tremblay had provided his cell number, and Greg considered using it to carry out his first promise, telling the policeman that he was at the house but Jay had not appeared. He wanted to get *that* task out of the way. But calling at such an hour, without an apparent emergency, would seem strange. If the police got the slightest suspicion of what was happening, they'd have no choice but to get involved. Jay had made it clear what he would do then.

Greg wished he could at least talk to his sister. After all, half of the money being extorted belonged to her, and later he would have to find a way to repay it. But none of what was going on could be explained to her right now. Nor could Jill be expected to keep quiet. So there was no comfort to be had there.

In the end, he went to bed. He tossed and turned for most of the night, lost in endless loops of guilt and recrimination, relieved only by dire scenarios of what would happen if anything went wrong. This ground on for hours until, as dawn was breaking, he fell at last into a fitful slumber. But instead of respite, all this brought was disconnected dreams, images of blood and money and the dark depths of the river.

THIRTY-TWO

Waking, he discovered that it was nearly 9:00 AM He got up, feeling as though, even without benefit of booze, he had a rotten hangover. He showered, shaved and had coffee, but couldn't stomach the idea of breakfast.

But now he could perform his first task for ensuring the women's safety. He put through the call to Sergeant Tremblay, waiting apprehensively while it rang, hoping that his nervousness wouldn't show. The phone rang several times and then, just as Greg was about to give up, the policeman answered. He sounded in a hurry, which was all to the good. Greg made his report, saying that he was at the house and—truthfully—that Jay had never arrived. Tremblay, mind obviously elsewhere, thanked him, told him to hang tough and, by inference, not to bother him again unless there was something to report. That was that. By 10:00 AM, Greg was on his way to the bank in Duncan.

With no appointment, he had to wait half an hour to see Herb Wilshire, the manager, but he didn't mind. It gave him time to settle, assuming the serious but relaxed demeanour necessary for the business in hand. Not that he expected any problems. As executor, he had a perfect right to transfer any sum of money he chose from the estate's account, and in any form he chose—including cash. Though his request might occasion surprise, it could hardly be refused.

When he entered the office, to be greeted by Herb, with his big smile and bigger handshake, Greg had the feeling that he had almost been expected. After the customary small talk, beneath the familiar decoration of the Walter Lothian seascape, Wilshire leaned back and said, "Well, Greg, what can I do for you?"

From his pocket, Greg produced a cheque, drawn on the estate, which he'd already prepared. Trying to sound as if this were the most natural thing in the world, he passed it across Herb's desk and said, "I'd like to get cash for this, please."

"Of course," Herb said, picking up the cheque. "But you needn't have bothered waiting to see me about . . ." He stopped, as he realized what he was looking at. His eyebrows went up almost comically. "Oh—I see . . . You *did* say cash?"

"That's right." Greg tried for a casual smile. "Under the circumstances, I figured I'd better not just walk up to the teller, if you see what I mean."

Herb's eyebrows had not yet descended. "Seven hundred grand in cash," he breathed. "What do you . . . I mean, why would . . ." He coughed and adjusted his face. "Of course, there's no reason why you *shouldn't* . . . Big payrolls used to be done regularly this way. But I can't remember when I last . . . What about a cashier's cheque? It's just like actual money, you know, and much safer."

Greg shook his head. "I understand. But it has to be cash."

Herb scanned the cheque, blinking, as if he were having difficulty in taking it in. Then he said, "Greg—I hope . . ."

"Yes?"

"Well, this is so unusual . . . I mean, are you at liberty to tell me why you need so much cash?"

"Not really. Sorry."

"It's just—there are so many scams around these days. Temptations for gambling. Criminals using every trick to get their hands on people's precious assets. I can't help remembering what happened to your parents."

Greg shook his head brusquely. "Thanks for the concern, Herb, but it's nothing like that. Now—it's my guess a branch this size doesn't have that kind of cash on hand, right?"

"Er—correct."

"How long will it take?"

Pulling himself together, Herb shrugged. "I could have it in by tomorrow, probably. What would you like?"

"Pardon?"

"Denominations."

"Oh—hundreds would be best, I should think."

"Hundreds, all right." Herb made a note on the cheque, grinning weakly. "At least getting it home won't need a moving van."

Greg smiled politely in return. "Quite. When tomorrow could you have it ready?"

"Would noon be satisfactory?"

Greg rose, looking directly at his father's painting, a reminder of the historic sale, whose proceeds were in the process of being highjacked. "Noon would be fine," he said resignedly, and left the office.

THIRTY-THREE

When he got back to the house, he changed his clothes and felt suddenly ravenous. Only then did he realize how much tension he'd been under. Should something have prevented his quickly obtaining the cash, he dared not think of the consequences. But that hadn't happened. His main task now was to make sure that Jay was reassured, to apprise him of progress and the timetable. Surely the guy would be glad to know he only had to wait twenty-four hours, rather than the two days Greg had envisaged. And with the news that everything was going as planned, Jay would relax and not be tempted to harm anyone.

It would have been a relief to deliver the message by phone, but Greg had been instructed to bring it personally. So, having crammed down a hasty snack, he set off through the woods in the direction of the Lynley house.

Reaching the place where in the past he'd been greeted by Hatch, he was assaulted by morbid images from the night before. The more confident mood, brought on by his earlier success, evaporated. For a moment, he'd been lulled into thinking that, though frightening, this was, after all, just a business transaction. But it wasn't. He was now operating in the jungle, where nothing in his background or character was likely to help. There was no fairness here. No rules. And although Jay was getting what he wanted, this didn't mean things would necessarily be okay. To say the very least, Greg was going to have to keep his wits about him.

Coming in sight of the house, he saw that Lucy's car was still there, but the van was gone. What did that mean? Probably only that it had been hidden, out of sight of any casual callers. Jay was certainly shrewd enough to have thought of that. There was a big double garage to one side of the house, which Greg remembered had been used as a workshop. One of the doors was ajar and when he got closer, sure enough, he glimpsed the van inside.

Mercifully, the front stoop of the house had been cleaned. The bloodstains were gone, as was the dog. But this probably hadn't been done for reasons of sensitivity. More likely, as with hiding the van, it was simply to make the place look normal.

Only after he climbed the steps did Greg realize that his arrival had not been unmonitored. Trev was in the hall, arms folded, as immobile as a Coast Salish carving, regarding him through the window, and he opened the door smartly, like a concierge. It might have been amusing—except that it wasn't.

Lucy and her mother were nowhere to be seen. Jay was alone in the living room, lounging in the chair into which he'd plunged his knife. "Hi, partner," he said amiably. "How'd it go?"

Greg took a breath. "Where are the women?"

"I asked you a question," Jay replied, amiable no more.

"And I asked *you* one. Look, Jay—we're not talking until I've seen they're all right."

"And you're not seeing a fucking thing, buddy, till you've told me what I want to know."

Stalemate. Standing up to Jay was satisfying, but it was childish and dangerous. "Tomorrow," he said heavily. "I've arranged to pick up the cash at noon."

Jay grinned, unconsciously rubbing the dent in his head. "Sweet! How hard was that, eh? The bank bastards give you any grief?"

"No. It's my money. Why should they?"

"Okay. Get it here pronto tomorrow, and maybe *I* won't give you any either."

Jay nodded to Trev, who was standing behind Greg. The big native backed off, motioning Greg to follow. They moved along the corridor to the door of Shirl's room. Greg knocked. There was no reply, but he opened the door anyway. "Hello, it's Greg," he called, and went in.

The older woman was in bed, eyes closed, seemingly asleep. Her daughter, fully clothed, was lying on top of the covers beside her. A tray with the remains of a meal was on the bedside table. As Greg entered, Lucy got up hastily. Though her face was calm, her eyes were dark and hollow.

Greg felt an unexpectedly powerful surge of emotion: partly relief, partly guilt, but largely a sensation of such tenderness that it brought an embarrassing blurriness to his vision. The need to hide this caused him to speak more brusquely than he intended. "Hello, Lucy, how are you? How's your mum?"

"We're okay," Lucy said.

Shirl opened her eyes and gave him a weak smile.

"Good," he said quietly. "I just wanted you to know I've made arrangements to get the money."

Lucy's relieved look included a quick glance at her mother.

"And sooner than I expected. I'm picking it up tomorrow at noon. I'll bring it straight here—and then all this will be over."

"Thank God."

Lucy went to the bed, talking softly to Shirl, who nodded, lifting her hand toward Greg in a gesture of what appeared to be thanks, but so weak he felt freshly worried. When Lucy returned, he whispered, "She's not good, is she?"

Lucy sighed, shaking her head

"But she's worse since . . . Does she need a doctor?"

Lucy gave him her straight look. "Is there any chance of that happening?"

Greg lowered his eyes. "I shouldn't think so. Not till—you know."

"Then stop asking dumb questions. Please, just get back with the money as quick as you can."

Greg nodded glumly, then noticed a flutter of movement on the bed. Shirl was beckoning. With a glance at Lucy, he went to her mother. "I'm so sorry, Mrs. Lynley," he said.

Shirl shook her head, the action small but determined. "Never mind, dear," she replied. "And take no notice of Lucy. She's just worried about me."

"I know. But it's my fault . . ."

"No, dear. It's no one's. Not even that greedy young man's, really. The world makes us what we are, long before we do foolish things. Anyway, don't worry about that. What I wanted to ask you is about Hatch."

"I'm so sorry . . . "

"No, *listen*—this has been on my mind, and they won't let Lucy out to do it. Greg, please—would you bury our poor dear guy?"

After some hunting, he found a spade. Hatch's body was where it had been callously tossed, behind the shed. Greg hadn't asked where they wanted the grave, so he followed his impulse, which was to dig it in the place that he most associated with the joyous beast; hefting the spade, he headed in the direction of the river.

This was fifty yards from the house and screened by a grove of trees. Passing through these, he came to a sandy bank leading down to the water, the sight of which induced a feeling of déjà vu. Staring at it for a while brought the answer: this was where he'd come ashore after his wild plunge into the river, and where Hatch had discovered him, likely saving his life.

The perfect place.

He set to, digging a hole big enough in a spot well above high water. Then he rooted in the workshop where the van was hidden and found an old carpet. Mindfully, trying to avoid looking at the dreadful wound, he wrapped Hatch in his improvised shroud. The sad body felt pitifully light. Having secured the bundle, he carried it from behind the shed, only then realizing he was not alone. The big native, Trev, in his usual totem-like posture, was standing nearby. Greg stopped and their eyes met. Then something unexpected occurred: without changing expression, Trev gave a quick, almost formal nod. Then he turned and walked into the house.

Bearing his burden, Greg returned to the river. As gently as he could, he placed the still-wrapped dog in the freshly dug grave. While he shovelled back the earth, the words Shirl had used earlier came back to him. "Sorry, poor dear guy," he muttered. "Yeah, sorry, poor dear guy."

As he put down the spade and turned away, he saw something he hadn't noticed earlier. A short distance from the grave, sitting upright and half hidden by brush, was a green canoe. Greg remembered Lucy's father being a keen outdoorsman, but surely it couldn't have been there very long. Then, remembering the recent storm, he figured it must have been washed up. Observing the water, deceptively calm in the bright afternoon, he remembered his own ordeal with awful clarity. *God*, he thought, *I hope some poor sod wasn't in this when it went over.* He glanced about, half expecting to see yet another mouldering victim of the river's caprice, but there was nothing. Of course there was nothing. The turmoil that—due to his own actions—had invaded his once peaceful existence was now providing its final insult: paranoia.

Not wishing to see the Lynley house again, until he could set its prisoners free, Greg followed the riverbank back to his own property.

The rest of the day, the night and the first hours of the following morning passed at a pace that, on Greg's internal clock, felt like a slow year. But at last, showered and dressed, and as physically calm as possible for a man half mad with suppressed anxiety, he was in the car, heading into Duncan. Beside him was a gym bag, old but solid, big enough for the job at hand.

He parked in the bank lot at five minutes before noon and headed inside. Apparently, he was expected, for after introducing himself, he was ushered immediately into Herb Wilshire's office. It was empty, but he was told that the manager would be joining him momentarily.

Greg seated himself, trying to stop his feet from tapping with impatience, eyes turning inevitably to his father's painting. *Wow, Dad,* he mused. *If only you could see this. Seven hundred grand of your hard-earned cash in exchange for Lucy Lynley. What would you think of that?*

His thoughts were interrupted by the entrance of Herb Wilshire. The manager was followed by another bankerly looking man in a sober suit, presumably some kind of security person who, once Greg had his money, would be charged with seeing him safely off the premises.

"Good afternoon, Greg," Herb Wilshire said, his smile and handshake even more determined than usual. "Right on time, I see."

"Of course," Greg said. And then, too excited to indulge further in formalities. "Do you have the money?"

"Yes, yes. It's all ready for you to check and sign for. But—er—before you do that . . ."

He turned to other man, who had been standing quietly in the background. With surprise, Greg realized that the manager's face had gone bright red.

"Greg," Herb Wilshire said, "this is Sergeant Doakes of the RCMP. It seems that he'll need a few minutes of your time."

THIRTY-FOUR

"I'm sorry to cause you any embarrassment," Herb Wilshire said. "It's so long since I've disbursed such a large cash sum, you see. Until you'd left yesterday, I didn't realize how much the rules have changed."

"What rules?" Greg said numbly. "I don't understand. This is my family's money. I have a perfect right to . . ."

The man who'd been introduced as Sergeant Doakes cleared his throat. "Your rights are not an issue, Mr. Lothian. We know the money's yours. I'm only here to save you the trouble of coming to the station. And to ask a couple of questions."

"Really? And what would they be?" Greg said woodenly, though he knew where this was going.

"I should leave you two alone," the manager said.

"No, stay, sir," the sergeant said. "You need to hear this too." He turned back to Greg. "What Mr. Wilshire said about rules amounts to this: particularly since 9/11, when terrorism became such a factor in our lives, but also because of the war on drugs—not to mention money laundering and income tax evasion—we need to keep track of large sums of money. To know not only where they came from but also—as in your case—where they are going. Do you understand me, sir?"

Greg just stared.

"Of course, there's nothing, legally, to prevent a citizen possessing as much cash as he or she desires," Doakes continued. "But in the world today, where there's increasingly little need for banknotes at all, the main users of cash are, unfortunately, the criminal or radical elements. Knowing your family, Mr. Lothian, Mr. Wilshire was certain your own reasons for wanting so much paper money must be legitimate. But he also realized it was his duty to contact us—so that *everyone* could rest easy. Am I making sense here?"

Greg managed a nod. The movement was miniscule, because his whole body seemed frozen, but the policeman's sharp eye apparently caught it.

"Mr. Lothian," he concluded quietly, "to clear this matter up, so you can carry on with your business and we can all be on our way—why exactly do you need such a large sum in banknotes?"

There was a long silence. Sergeant Doakes and Herb Wilshire watched him, waiting. Greg, who had known in his heart the minute the policeman had been introduced that it was over, now grew strangely calm. "I need it," he said quietly, "for a most important reason."

"And what is that?"

"To save the lives of my friends."

By 1:00 PM, with the conference—minus Herb Wilshire—moved to Sergeant Doakes' office at the Duncan detachment of the RCMP, Greg was still talking. At 1:30 PM, looking grim under his red brush cut, Sergeant Tremblay of the Victoria police arrived.

Greg had no idea how much the Duncan RCMP knew about the operation their colleagues had been conducting with the cops in Victoria. He didn't offer any more information than necessary about his previous dealings with Tremblay, and from what he could understand of the police exchanges, some of which were conducted out of his hearing, Tremblay didn't go too deeply into that either. All that was settled was that he, Greg, was an innocent citizen who'd got caught up in a police sting operation, unwittingly putting himself—and, by catastrophic mischance, his neighbours—in jeopardy.

Without giving details as to how Jay had become involved with Greg, Tremblay made no bones about the danger posed by the extortionist, painting a grim picture of a criminal perfectly capable of carrying out his threats against the Lynleys. His sidekick, Trev, was known to the local police: a troublemaker so violent that, after half killing the son of the local band chief, he'd been thrown off the reserve.

When this was established, Greg, who'd been growing desperate as time passed, could hold back no longer. "So you see," he interrupted finally, "there's only one solution!"

All eyes turned to him. "And what is that?" Sergeant Doakes asked.

"What I was about to do—take him the money."

All heads, save that of Sergeant Tremblay, began to shake, so Greg continued quickly. "Listen—those women are hostages, right? You people must know about that kind of situation. And you've heard what Jay's like. The only way Lucy and her mother will be safe is if he gets the money. And the only one who can take it to him is me. He hates cops. He said that if he even smells one, he'll kill someone. And I've seen what he's capable of. Right now, he thinks he's scared me badly enough not to tell anyone. And he was right; I wasn't going to. But now you know. So it's vital that you keep out of sight, at least till he's got what he wants and leaves. That's it. The only way. Oh—and he expected me back hours ago, so please, I *must* get going."

They didn't like the idea that he, a civilian, should be allowed to go in alone. But it was his money, his life to risk and his responsibility. In the end, no one could argue with that. Tremblay had made no mention of Greg's history of taking the law into his own hands, but Greg knew, which was more than enough. If for no other reason, he had to try to make things right.

At 3:00 PM, two hours after he should have been back, the plan was finalized. Alone, Greg would return to the Lynley house, bearing the seven hundred thousand dollars. By then, well concealed, the police would have sealed off the area, ready to grab Jay and Trev the moment they abandoned their captives and attempted to depart.

Assuming abandonment was all that Jay had in mind.

As Greg was about to leave, Sergeant Tremblay drew him aside. "You're some piece of work, fella," he said with a quiet smile.

"I think we already had that conversation."

"Yeah, well, just so's you know—I reckon you're pretty brave, too."

"Pretty stupid, more likely."

Tremblay grinned. "Maybe. Anyway, in case of emergency, don't forget you can call me."

Greg was surprised. "You're sticking around?"

"You kidding? Wouldn't miss it. This isn't my patch, but the horsemen let me tag along. Professional courtesy and all that."

"What about that thing in Victoria?"

Tremblay looked surprised. "Oh, that! Haven't had a chance to tell you. It went down last night. We picked up the lot of them. If this hadn't happened, we'd have come for your guy tomorrow anyway. Good luck, Mr. Lothian."

THIRTY-FIVE

He began his drive back to the house almost immediately. Not far behind, a whole contingent of hastily assembled police followed, ready to surround the two properties as soon as he went in. More officers would be approaching from the other direction, where the west end of Riverbottom joined the Old Lake Cowichan Road, effectively sealing off the whole area. When Jay got his money and tried to make his departure, he would walk into a trap.

No one knew when that departure would be. Most likely, cash in hand, he'd want to get out right away. But that couldn't be counted on. Smart and tricky, he might prefer to wait until dark. Either way, his welcoming committee would be waiting.

Greg's most important job was not just to deliver the cash, but to make sure that Jay remained calm and, above all, unsuspicious. On the floor beside him was the gym bag containing seven thousand hundred-dollar bills. It was surprising how little space that much money took up, the equivalent of a load of paperback novels, heavy but quite manageable. Despite his tension earlier, the sight of so much cash—a rarity in this electronic age—had made Greg strangely exhilarated. He hoped that the same thing would happen to Jay, so he'd just want to grab it and run. Greg thought about that wonderful moment all the way home.

Reaching his gate, he drove in and closed it behind him,

maintaining a careful façade of normalcy. He was sure he must be anxiously awaited. And though he saw no one, it was unlikely that his return would not be observed. Anticipating this, the police had arranged to keep well back out of sight.

The driveway, winding through the trees to the house, was peaceful in the warm afternoon light. He passed the tree where, an age ago, he'd set the tripwire that had signalled the approach of Molinara. If he'd had one ounce of foresight as to how the world would unravel after that, he'd surely have run screaming into the night. But he hadn't, so here he was, doing his best to put an end to the game he'd so rashly begun. "Oh, man," he muttered, as he left the car, carrying his bag of riches. "For once, just let me get it right."

There was no time to waste. He'd hurry to the Lynleys and deliver the money right away. He headed around the house in the direction of the well-trodden path to the next property. Coming in sight of the studio, he stopped dead and nearly dropped his precious bag. In the breezeway, standing like a statue and staring directly at him, was Trev.

He approached the huge native, raising the gym bag nervously. "Got it," he said, trying hard not to sound completely unhinged. "Sorry it took so long."

Trev didn't say a word. With a brief head gesture, somehow conveying *Shut up, follow me* and *You're lucky I don't break your neck*, he began walking. Greg hurried after him, like a kid following the school bully. Already it was clear how important it had been to keep the police presence hidden. By the way Trev had materialized, he'd probably been watching for quite some time.

So far, so good. But as they travelled the path to the Lynley house, he began to get increasingly nervous. What if Jay sensed that something was wrong, that another double-cross, as he called it, was in the works? To calm himself, he decided to chat with his escort. Catching up with Trev, he tapped the money bag, sharply enough that the native looked around.

"So what's your cut of all this going to be, Trev?" Greg asked. Predictably, Trev didn't answer, so Greg continued, "Because, whatever it is, I promise to double it later, if you do just one thing for me now."

Still, Trev said nothing. But after a few more paces his head turned, and his expression had just the smallest hint of questioning.

"All I want," Greg said, "is for you to make sure that Jay doesn't hurt the women."

Nothing. Trev just lumbered on. Was he interested? Was he considering it? Who could tell? And soon it was too late for speculation. They'd come to the end of the path and were in the open, heading for the house.

The only difference in the scene was that the van had reappeared. That was a good sign, indicating that the criminals were seriously ready to leave. Then, as the front porch came into view, one more change was revealed. Beside the door, a chair had been placed. On it sat Jay. As they got closer, it could be seen that in his hand, instead of the knife, was a gun. This one did not look like a toy.

When they reached the bottom of the steps, Jay stood up. Without warning, he raised the gun, pointing it directly at Greg's chest. He gasped, instinctively lifting the bag in a futile gesture of protection. Jay gave a low laugh, shifting his aim to between Greg's eyes. Looking directly down the dark void of the barrel, Greg thought, *This is it. He's got what he wanted and I'm dead.*

Then Jay made a sound like an explosion, and blew invisible smoke from the gun barrel before putting it in his pocket. "What the fuck kept you, buddy?" he asked.

Greg's horror turned to anger, then to relief. At least this bit of sick comedy had provided cover for the first anxious moments. Appearing flustered now was only natural. "The Brinks delivery was late," he said, quoting a preplanned script. "The money wasn't ready. Sorry—but I came as quick as I could."

Jay gave his characteristic shrug, then extended his hand. Greg mounted the steps and handed over the bag. The other man took it without a word, turned on his heel and walked into the house.

That was it. No fuss, no ceremony—certainly no thanks. But who cared? He was still alive. As soon as Jay went inside, Greg followed. When he arrived in the hall, Jay had already vanished, presumably to check out his loot. Well, it was all there. That wouldn't take long to establish. Now Greg's only concern was the women.

He found them in Shirl's room, in almost the same position as the day before. The older woman was propped on pillows, looking a little better. But Lucy's anxious eyes consumed him as she slid off the bed and hurried to him.

"It's okay," Greg said. "I got it. He's counting it now."

"Oh, thank God!" She almost fell against him, alternately hugging and patting him in relief. "That's wonderful. Thank you. We're so . . ." She broke off and hurried to the bed. "Mum, did you hear? It's over."

"Yes, dear," Shirl replied. "Thank you, Greg. I don't know how we'll ever be able to repay you."

He made appropriate rejoinders, saying that the whole thing was his fault anyway, knowing also that it was far from over. If Jay was satisfied with his prize, and had no cruel games planned, he'd still probably want to restrain his prisoners so they couldn't raise the alarm after his departure. Assuming that was what he had in mind and not something more permanent.

Greg was in a quandary as to whether to tell the others about the police. Though it was good news, it could also cause a lot of anxiety. Probably it would be best to wait till they were safely alone to reveal that help would soon be on the way. He had just reached that conclusion when Trev entered the bedroom.

Ignoring the women, he gestured for Greg to come with him. Jay was waiting in the living room, in his usual armchair. The open gym bag was on the floor at his feet. "You did good, partner," Jay said with a grin. "It's all there."

"Of course," Greg replied quickly. "I said I'd get it. I kept my part of the bargain. Now, please, will you just take it and leave us alone?"

Jay pursed his lips and glanced into his lap. Greg noticed that a stack of bills lay there. Jay picked up the money and held it out to Trev. "There you go, big guy. Down payment. Count it and get outa here."

Trev took the money but didn't count it. He just stuffed the thick wad in his pocket and left. A moment later the front door slammed, and soon there came the sound of an engine starting. Through the window, Greg caught a glimpse of the van, heading down the driveway.

He felt relief, knowing it to be premature. Jay's "muscle" had departed, but *he* was the dangerous one. The crisis wouldn't be over until he was gone too. As if reading his thoughts, Jay rose, picked up the money bag and said, "Well, partner, I guess you're wondering when I'm gonna fuck off too, eh?"

Greg shrugged, wondering at the same time how long it would be before Trev was apprehended. The roadblock would no doubt be well out of sight of the Lynley gate. Even if Jay followed right along—presumably in Lucy's car—he wouldn't know what had happened till too late. God, the whole thing could be over in minutes.

This fond hope, however, was dashed almost instantly. "You're not getting rid of me yet," Jay grinned, glancing at his watch. "I reckon I'm just gonna relax a while. Maybe have a bite, before I hit the road."

Damn! Greg was disappointed but not surprised. He'd thought earlier that Jay might wait until dark before leaving. Well, the cops were prepared for that too. It was arranged that they would do nothing till he appeared. Later, Greg might even be able to get through a call to Tremblay, explaining the situation. But for now, they'd just have to hang on. Their captor seemed content. As long as he could be kept that way until his departure, everything could yet turn out all right.

"In that case," Greg said quietly, "perhaps I can get Lucy to fix an early supper."

"Good thinking." Jay checked his watch again. "Tell your lady to go to it."

Lucy made the meal while Greg was allowed to keep Shirl company. He'd have liked to make a call to Tremblay, but since there was no immediate emergency, he didn't want to risk being caught. Also, to phone in front of Shirl would have involved revealing the police presence, knowledge he still considered best kept to himself. So he tried to be cheerful, seeing to Shirl's needs and reassuring her as best he could.

It was 5:30 PM when Lucy had the food ready; she had fried sausages and cooked up vegetables and pasta in her usual skillful manner. She took a tray to her mother, then the others sat down to eat like a peculiar sort of family, Greg thought. Jay, with his bag of money nearby, ate calmly. The others picked away, trying to hide their impatience. But it was in fact Jay who, several times during the meal, looked at his watch. Then, when his plate was empty, the young man put down his utensils neatly and checked his watch one last time.

"Six o clock," Jay said cheerfully. "Well, guys, I guess that about clinches it."

"Clinches what?" Greg asked.

"Oh, I think you know," Jay replied. He got up from the table and produced a cellphone. "Trev had strict instructions to call me as soon as he got into Duncan. He thought that was to set up a meeting for later. What he *didn't* know was that I'd still be here—waiting to see if he made it out okay."

Greg's insides went cold. "What are you talking about?"

Jay grinned, his expression edged in ice. "Bait! Big Trev was bait—which your cop buddies, who I suspected might be waiting out there, have swallowed whole. Letting me know—partner—that you've double-crossed me again."

THIRTY-SIX

After the first dreadful moment, what really caught Greg's attention was the expression on Lucy's face. More than simple shock, it was as if, deep down, she'd always known Greg would fail them. Whether she actually believed this didn't matter; the thought made him abandon all pretense. "Okay! But it wasn't my fault," he said desperately. "I didn't go to the police. They came to me."

"Bullshit!"

"No! It was the *money*. That large an amount of cash made the bank manager suspicious. He told the cops, and when I went to get it, they were waiting. I had to tell them what it was for. I had no option."

"And I've got no option but to waste you," Jay snarled, raising his gun. "You're fucking dead, buddy."

"No!" Greg cried, backing off, almost tripping over Lucy, who had jumped up and now moved between the two men.

"Don't do it, Jay," Lucy said steadily.

Appalled, Greg tried to pull Lucy from in front of him. But instead of shooting, Jay laughed. "Shit," he said, "this bitch has got more guts than you."

"No, *listen*!" Lucy replied, with such intensity that Jay's gun wavered. "If the police *have* caught your friend, they must be close by. If they hear shooting, they'll know there's no point in waiting anymore. They'll probably storm the place. Have you thought of that?"

Jay obviously hadn't. Nor had Greg, for that matter. Before either could respond, Lucy walked toward the door. "While you do," she said firmly, "I'm going to my mother. This has nothing to do with her or me. It never did. But if you kill us, Jay, the police will do the same to you. The only use we are is alive. Greg, I'm sorry. If Jay has any sense, he'll give up. But, in any case . . . you'll just have to work it out."

Lucy gave Greg a last long look, an expression that somehow managed to convey sorrow and resignation but also encouragement. Then she turned down the hall. A moment later, in the dull silence that followed, came the sound of a closing door.

"Now that's one ballsy bitch," Jay said at last.

Greg, who was thinking the same thing, nodded agreement. "And she was right. This has nothing to do with her or her mother." He gulped mentally, but went on. "You've got to believe I didn't mean for the police to get involved. It's my fault for starting this thing in the first place, and I blame myself for that. But I've done the best I could since then. And you *have* got your money. Why don't you just take it and go? I won't try to stop you."

That at least made Jay laugh. "No shit! The only thing you could stop right now, partner, is a fucking bullet."

"I only meant I won't try to give the alarm."

"Oh, yeah? Think I believe that?"

"You don't have to. You could tie me up and . . ."

He stopped. He'd had a sudden idea. It was dangerous, and could put them in an even worse position, but it was at least something to bargain with: a course of action which, even to the angry Jay, might seem an advantage, and better than creating mayhem. It could also backfire. Just because Jay got something didn't mean he'd return the favour. Lucy had stopped him cold once with the reminder that shooting would likely bring in the police. But shooting wasn't the only way he could do harm, as poor Hatch's body had shown. Jay was paranoid and probably crazy—which also meant that they had little to lose. On balance, it was worth a try.

Having come rapidly to this conclusion, Greg reached into his pocket and brought out his cellphone. He said calmly, "If you promise not to harm the women, there's a way I could buy you some time."

Jay stared from the phone to Greg. "What are you trying to pull now?"

"Nothing. If you look in the phone menu, you'll see the number of Sergeant Tremblay from the Victoria police."

That surprised Jay. "*He's* out there?"

"Yes. When the RCMP wanted to know why I needed all that cash, I had to bring him in to prove I wasn't a crook like . . . well, you know. He told me to phone him in case of emergency."

"No fucking shit!" Jay grabbed the phone, examining it closely.

"By now they'll have caught Trev," Greg continued, "just like you figured. But what they *don't* know is that you're wise to them. If I call the sergeant and tell him that we're okay, that you don't know anything's gone wrong but you're cautious and don't plan to leave till, say the early hours, when everything's quiet, then they'll hold off. And that'll give you time to escape."

Jay was still examining the phone. He gave Greg a look, if not of respect, at least of true surprise. "You're a slippery bastard."

"No. I just don't want you to hurt anyone. Anything's worth that."

With a sudden savage move, Jay shoved the phone back across the table. "Including being a lying asshole."

"I'm not lying," Greg said desperately. "Look, I can prove it. If you call that number on the phone, you can hear Tremblay identify himself. Then I'll take the phone and tell him the story. You'll be able to hear the whole thing. And since the police have no idea that you're on to them, he'll believe it. Come on, it'll work. What do you say?"

Passing his gun from hand to hand, Jay began to pace. Eventually he said, "If the cops did keep their distance, what makes you believe I can get out of here?"

There was a pause. At last Greg said, "Well, I've been thinking. Since you set Trev up, on the chance he *was* caught, you must have had something in mind. No point in having a warning system without an alternative plan."

Jay's suspicious expression morphed into a grin that was almost effusive. "Shit," he chuckled, "what a waste."

"What do you mean?"

"You and me. With your brains and my smarts, we'd have made awesome partners. If you want to know—I have got another way out. So—okay. Phone your cop buddy."

Needing no further urging, Greg picked up the phone. He handed it to Jay, who pocketed his gun and activated Tremblay's number. Almost immediately, a voice, audible even to Greg, said, "Hello, Tremblay."

Jay handed the phone to Greg.

"Hello, Sergeant," Greg said, talking low as if he feared to be overheard, "this is Greg. Did you catch the first guy?"

Tremblay said that they had. Carefully, never taking his eyes off his captor's face, Greg told the story that they had agreed on. Tremblay seemed pleased, and both Greg and Jay could hear the sergeant making asides to the other officers, conveying the news. Assured that the captives were all right, the police would sit tight until either Jay appeared or Greg called back.

When it was over, Jay looked pleased. "Okay, that's taken care of. Good thinking, Mr. Lothian. Like I said, we could have been real good partners."

That old song again. Did he honestly mean it? No, it was probably just his weird way of making conversation. Greg wanted to go to Lucy, to tell her the news, that a sort of bargain appeared to have been made, that things were looking up. But he figured he'd better not appear to take too much for granted just yet. This was a volatile guy, and the cooler he played it, the safer all round.

"I don't know what help I could have been in the sort of things you do," he said, considering it useless, not to mention pathetic, to try to lie. "But I certainly admire your resourcefulness."

"What do you mean?" Jay asked, his tone changing.

"Having an escape plan. Very clever."

"Gee, thanks. And I bet you'd just love to know what it is, eh?"

"No, I . . ." Greg began, then stopped short, as he realized that Jay's gun had reappeared. Since he was seated at the table while Jay was standing, the weapon, held casually at waist level, was pointed directly at Greg's head.

"You're doing it again, aren't you, partner," Jay whispered, beginning to circle. "Figuring how to double-cross me."

Greg felt deathly cold. As Jay moved behind him, he could feel, like an actual physical caress, the aiming point of the gun tracking around his head, from eye to ear to the nape of his neck. He wanted to look back, to see what was happening, to register if Jay's finger was beginning to exert pressure on the trigger, but he didn't dare. Any move now could set off a fatal counter-move behind him. If only he stayed perfectly still, this moment of horror and yet of continued existence might last forever. But it could not; he knew that. And before it ended, there was one thing that had to be said.

"Whatever you think you have to do," he heard a voice that seemed to be his own saying, "please don't hurt the women . . ."

Then something red and black and unbearably starry white exploded in his head—and there was nothing.

THIRTY-SEVEN

I'm dead. That was his first conviction, after dream-like thought processes coalesced into consciousness; then pain crowded in, letting him know with sour certainty that he was not. The throbbing was centred in the back of his head, radiating forward to the blood-tinged blackness behind his closed eyelids. But it wasn't only there. As his awareness expanded, he realized that his whole body ached—neck, torso, arms and legs—as if he'd been thrown down and rolled over by a bulldozer.

Christ, I've been in a car accident, he thought, and opened his eyes.

He was lying face down on a hardwood floor. That much he knew, because the shiny, grained surface was literally inches from his eyes. The fact was, he could only see with one of them, since the other was flattened against the floor, the most comfortless pillow he had ever known. Gingerly, he tried to relieve the pressure by moving his head, but found that he could not. Since he was on his stomach, he needed to roll. However, when he tried to move, he discovered that both sets of limbs were tied, arms securely behind his back, ankles to each other.

This information was followed by a sickening kaleidoscope of returning memory. His painful resting place was the Lynley living room, where he'd been—not shot, apparently—bludgeoned and hogtied.

Better than being dead.

Then Greg had another thought. It didn't decrease his discomfort, but made enduring it easier: if Jay had gone to the trouble of merely immobilizing him, rather than using his gun, he was unlikely to have done worse to the women.

That sent a surge of energy through Greg's tightly trussed frame. It gave him the strength to lift and twist his body enough to be able to roll onto his side, and he found himself gazing across the strange terrain of the floor. A foot in front of him, like a huge, squashed insect, was the ruin of what had been his cellphone. Beyond, at the limit of his vision, was the entrance to the hall. Somewhere beyond, please God in no worse straits than himself, were the women. If that were the case, Lucy would probably be all right. But what about her mother?

"Lucy!" The word croaked out, like the call of a half-strangled frog. Even should she be alert and listening, she was unlikely to hear. He tried again, with no better results, and decided that calling was futile. But lying passively and waiting for eventual release wasn't an option either.

Now that he was on his side, he discovered that, with great difficulty, he could roll right over onto his back. He drew up his knees and, though experiencing considerable pain from stiffened muscles, managed to sit up.

Only then could he see that his legs were bound not by rope but by a thick winding of silver duct tape. His arms, behind him, were presumably secured the same way. He tried to tug them apart, but stopped at once; it felt as if he were straining against bands of steel. *Damn you, Jay*, he thought bitterly, then, remembering the alternative, began concentrating on what he needed to do to get free.

The first thing he found was that by extending his legs, then executing a sort of wriggle-and-pull motion with his rear end, he could move across the floor. The process was clumsy and painfully slow, but he made it to the couch. What to do then? He leaned his shoulder against the couch, pulling his legs up and attempting to get his head and the top of his body onto the level surface so he could use it as support; then he would twist around, get his bound legs under him, and thus stand. The first time he tried, his shoulder slipped off the couch and he fell back down, hitting his head a stunning crack on the floor and ending in a position almost identical to when he'd first become conscious. This time he really did curse; it was either that or burst into tears. Using rage as a goad, he started over, first turning onto his back, then sitting up again. Once more he leaned over the couch—this time with shoulder properly planted—then humped and heaved more of his upper torso onto the soft surface. He got his legs underneath him and at last, with a mighty twist of shoulders and back, managed to throw himself into a standing crouch. Straightening his creaking knees brought him fully upright.

He stood panting, leaning against the arm of the couch, fighting not just gravity but a change in blood pressure that made his head swim. For a moment he feared he would faint and collapse again. He closed his eyes and clenched his jaw, holding onto consciousness by sheer strength of will. Slowly, the dizziness receded and he opened his eyes again.

Now all he could think of was the women. "Lucy!" he called. "Lucy, can you hear me?" There was no reply. He had to get to her. But the only way he could move was by little jumps. The first leap gained mere inches and a stumble that almost sent him flying. But the next try was better, and soon he was making a slow but steady pace across the living room.

When he reached the hall, he changed his mind. Whatever condition Lucy and Shirl were in, he couldn't help them trussed up like a turkey. The first thing, obviously, was to get loose.

He turned back and examined the living room, spotting nothing he could use to free himself. The kitchen seemed a formidable detour, but it was a more likely place. He shuffle-hopped there in what felt like a minor eternity to begin his search. Of course, there were many implements, scissors, knives, et cetera, that were fine for cutting duct tape, if only there had been someone to help him.

What he needed, he realized, was something securely fixed, with protruding edges that could be used to lacerate the tape. The woodstove, standing in one corner, had some likely-looking sharp edges, but they all were too low, or on the wrong angle for his purpose. Then his eyes fixed on something close and simple. One end of the kitchen counter had a sharp corner, at what seemed just the right height. He hopped over to it and backed in. Yes, the position was perfect. He could rest his wrists against the counter and then, jigging up and down with his knees, rub the sharp corner against the imprisoning tape. He tried it—too strenuously the first time; the tape slipped off the corner and, in trying to keep his balance, he gouged the flesh of his wrist. The pain made him yell out, and he could feel wet warmth on his hands. But he recovered, repositioned his arms and started again.

At that moment, a long, low cry came from somewhere off in the house.

He stopped. Called out. Waited. The cry came again. But it was not a response. It was a signal of distress—and the only way he could help was by not letting it distract him from his task.

Ignoring all subsequent sounds, he set to work. With the taped area between his wrists held taut, he began to rub it against the sharp corner. Up, down, up, down. He had no idea of the effect, could neither see nor feel what was happening. All he could do was try to keep the point of resistance in place and continue rubbing. Soon his knees, which were doing most of the work, began to grow weary and then to ache like hell. The crack in his ass also tended to come in contact with the corner lower down, and the fabric of his pants grew hot with the friction. It seemed that before the tape wore through, he was going to wear a nasty groove in himself. But he kept going. He had to—*had to!*

Then, as he was growing desperate, he felt movement. It was in his wrists: not much, but definitely something. And it gave his failing will a boost. Up and down he went, putting more pressure on his binding. At last, in the midst of a down-thrust, the corner caught, then burst right through the tape. He twisted and jerked, and there came a dull tearing sound. He leaned back, applying outward elbow leverage while he thrust his arms down. There was a final rip, he fell forward on his knees—and his wrists parted.

For a moment, as the strain on his back and shoulders was released and his arms whipped around to the front, the pain was so excruciating that he was sure something must be broken. Crouching on the floor, his unleashed limbs dangling like dead things, the left wrist dripping blood, he again felt on the verge of fainting. But the worst of the pain passed swiftly, making way for the exhilaration of freedom.

Well, near-freedom. He still had to deal with his taped ankles, but with two good, if battered, hands, this took no time at all. Without leaving his knees, he could reach the knife block on the counter. He plucked out a knife, fumbled, and had to duck as it sailed over his head. More cautiously he extracted another and sliced through his last restraint. Dropping the knife and letting his head fall onto his chest, he gave one long, heartfelt exhalation of breath. He'd done it.

At that moment there came another dreadful moan.

"Christ!" Greg cried, scrambling to his feet. "Coming—*I'm coming!*"

In a shambling trot, he crossed the kitchen and hurried down the hall, heading for the source of the sound, which he guessed to be Shirl Lynley's bedroom. On the threshold he stopped, leaning against the door frame as he gazed at the scene inside.

Light came from just one source, a bed lamp, which cast long shadows across the room. On the bed lay Shirl Lynley. Her eyes were open, but she made no movement to register his arrival.

Lucy was seated nearby. Though within arm's length of her

mother, she could not reach her. Thick loops of tape fastened her body to the chair and her wrists to its arms. More loops secured her ankles. A thick piece of tape had been plastered across her lower face. Lucy's eyes were round and anguished, gazing across the unbridgeable gulf to her mother. From beneath the gag she again made the bone-chilling moan.

"*Lucy!*" Greg cried, and only then did she see him. She began to make gurgling sounds, nodding desperately in the direction of her mother.

Greg wasn't sure what she meant, but he did know what he had to do. Fetching the knife from the kitchen, he cut her free, wrists, ankles and the cruelly tight binding about her upper arms and chest. Immediately, her hands went to her face, clawing at it, muttering, then giving a harsh cry as she ripped the tape away.

"Mum," Lucy wailed. "Oh, Mum, Mum . . ."

Thrusting him aside, she came out of her chair, almost collapsing as her stiff limbs refused support, then staggering across the short distance to her mother.

"Mum," she cried, falling onto her knees beside the bed so that the faces of the two were inches apart. "Mum, it's all right. I'm here. Mum—I'm so sorry—Mum—please . . ."

Her voice faded. Greg saw clearly the transformation filtering through her body, the slow shift in attitude, signalling that her world had changed forever. Finally she spoke, the words as cold and clear as ice.

"She's dead!"

Greg's insides were colder than her words. He moved to Lucy, placing his hands gently on her sagging shoulders. "I'm sorry," he said softly. "I'm just so sorry."

There was silence and stillness for a long moment. Then, shocking him with her suddenness, Lucy shrugged his hands away and scrambled up. Her entire body was aquiver, her face a terrifying mask, eyes blazing, skin dead white, mouth a twisted slash in the raw redness where the tape had been ripped away.

"Coward!" she hissed. "This is your fault! Get out! *I never want to set eyes on you again.*"

THIRTY-EIGHT

Greg stumbled out into the night in a daze of self-revulsion and despair. Fleeing the house, he plunged into the concealing dark, with no idea where he was going, blindly, hopelessly, wishing that instead of poor Shirl, it had been himself taking the final journey into death. But even that desire seemed selfish and sad: being killed by Jay wouldn't have saved the others; it would merely have let him avoid his distress at their fate. So, even now, his remorse was all about his own discomfort, rather than Lucy's. He was a thoroughgoing asshole, no doubt about that.

His desperate passage took him across the open area by the house and into the woods, unaware of the transition until he blundered into a tree trunk and fell flat. Half stunned, he lay on a bed of damp leaves, wishing he could just keep sinking and disappear. Then there came another unpleasant phenomenon; in his mind's eye arose the pale and cantankerous face of his dad. *Well, are you surprised at what happened?* the vision taunted. *You always were a pathetic loser.*

Walter was as Greg had last seen him, glowering from the pillow in the hospital bed on that final night. The anger that had filled him then returned. *Don't call me a loser,* he retorted to the unwelcome shade. *If it hadn't been for your foul temper, both you and Mum would still be alive.*

And if you'd kept your eye on your wallet, none of this would have happened.

Be that as it may, you as good as killed her.

Get real! She was dying anyway.

At least I tried to do something to make things right. Better than throwing a stupid tantrum and breaking your hip.

And throwing away seven hundred thousand dollars of my bread wasn't stupid?

"It was the only decent thing I did," Greg replied, realizing that he was babbling out loud into the wet leaves. God, he *was* a loser, finding refuge in tit-for-tat blame fantasies starring his dead father, maudlin nonsense that would change nothing. There was only one clear course of action open to him now.

Sighing, he hauled himself to his feet. With little interest, he noticed a subtle change in the previously unbroken black. The tree he'd bumped into stood out as a lighter patch in the gloom. Dawn was approaching. Okay, that would make what he had to do all the easier.

Somewhere up ahead, through woods that were emerging from the receding night, was the Cowichan River. Part of his world since early childhood, the waterway had lately become a major player in the sad drama in which he was immersed. It had snatched his mother, provided a disposal chute for a villain and, during a wild storm, almost taken Greg himself to its soggy bosom. And now . . . ? Now it was time for it to do its last and best work.

Thoughtfully, wishing to be peaceful in what he'd decided were to be his last moments, Greg made his way through the trees. He saw he was nearing the place where he'd buried the dog. Well, that was appropriate, too. What better companion to see him off on his final journey? Quietly, he drifted on. By now the dawn light was brightening fast. At one point Greg paused, gazing upward through the branches to a patch of open sky, gray, tinged with palest pink. His dad would have done a bang-up job of depicting a sky like that. *Ornery old codger,* he mused. *But you sure could paint up a storm. Too bad about the money.* Then he turned his attention back to the river.

When at last he emerged on the bank, there was enough light to make a clear reflection on the smooth surface of the water. He gazed at the scene tranquilly—then noticed something new; off to the left, very still but unmistakable in silhouette, was the figure of a man.

Jay.

He was standing at the water's edge, looking downstream. Nearby, one end in the water, was a canoe.

Greg's jaw dropped in stupefied understanding. So *this* was the escape route that Jay had boasted the police would never think of, what he'd called his "back door." He'd hinted that Greg had reason to know it well, which was all too true. Greg even remembered noticing the canoe, but it had never occurred to him to make the connection. In wretched hindsight, the plan was obvious: if anything went wrong, if Jay became trapped while the police were guarding exits and watching highways, he'd simply slip away down the river. Probably he even had another vehicle stashed farther downstream. It was so neat and easy, only one puzzle remained: why had he delayed so long?

Abruptly, the figure by the shore came to life. Jay's head tilted to survey the pale sky, turned back to look at the river, nodded in what looked like satisfaction—and Greg had his answer. Of course! Since trying to navigate treacherous waters in the dark was an obvious recipe for disaster, Jay had been waiting for the dawn.

Amazement, admiration and outrage mingled in a surge of emotion so strong that Greg was momentarily paralyzed. Then, as the other man leaned forward, preparing to launch the canoe, the spell broke. Unbidden, unstoppable, a sound erupted from deep inside the watcher, a roar of pure, brilliant rage. Arms extended, hands reaching and flexing, he charged down the riverbank, intent on only one thing: to claw out the throat of this destroyer.

He'd covered perhaps a quarter of the distance by the time Jay made a surprised recovery. Whirling, he dipped his hand in his pocket. It reappeared and there was an explosion and a flash of flame.

Part of Greg's rampaging mind knew exactly what was happening. He even noted the whine of a bullet passing his ear. But it didn't stop him. Though he had recently contemplated suicide, his mortality was utterly irrelevant. All he wanted was to get his hands on Jay. Nothing else mattered.

The second shot very nearly put an end to everything. What felt like the kick of a heavy boot was delivered to his shoulder, spinning him sideways. He tottered, nearly went down, righted himself and rushed on. Now he was almost upon his adversary, feeling no pain, lost in the delicious anticipation of revenge. The next shot tore at his side, again making him stagger, but he'd reached his target. Crashing into Jay, his arms went out in a rugby tackle, batting the weapon away and propelling both of them into the water.

Struggling to keep his balance, Jay desperately tried to free his gun hand, but he lost his footing and collapsed backward. Greg on top, both men were half submerged. Thrashing, pummelling, Jay got his arm loose. He couldn't get the gun around to fire, so he used it as a club, repeating his earlier assault on his opponent's head. This time the blow wasn't so effective, merely glancing off Greg's forehead. Then the gun twisted out of Jay's fingers and fell in the river.

Stunned, Greg was aware that Jay had lost a major advantage. Renewing his attack, he began to throw punches, not skillful but with furious energy. His right fist finally connected solidly. This caused violent pain in his own shoulder, but he didn't care. Always a non-physical person, he was finding this brutality wonderfully satisfying. He kept pounding away, rewarded by the feel of his knuckles making contact with the other's eye.

Jay gave a yell and delivered a vicious blow, which, by good fortune, Greg managed to parry. Jay pulled away and scrambled upright in the water. Greg came after him, grabbing his clothing and using Jay to haul himself upright. Jay swung about and belted him between the eyes.

A universe of bright stars obscured Greg's vision. Before it had time to clear, Jay hit him again. Greg cursed and, ignoring the renewed blows, went for Jay's throat. The two were face to face, thumping and flailing, up to their knees in the water. Then Greg got in a lucky blow. He felt his knuckles land on Jay's jaw. The other man slipped and fell flat, plunging beneath the water.

The light was now strong enough to let Greg see the submerged figure. It was scrabbling about on the bottom, disoriented, making no attempt to rise. In deadly satisfaction, Greg backed off. *The bastard's drowning,* he thought, which seemed so appropriate that he laughed. But quickly came the knowledge that he couldn't let it happen. Pounding the man in a rage was one thing—coldly watching him drown quite another.

Angry but unable to resist, Greg moved in again. Jay was still beneath the surface, arms and legs moving vaguely, as if he were losing consciousness. Greg readied himself to pull the man up, aware of the blossoming agony in the various parts of him that had been pummelled, bludgeoned or shot. He'd better hurry, he realized, or he was going to fail in this task too. Breathing deeply, he leaned down and grasped the back of the drowning man's jacket.

It was as though Jay had been awaiting that moment. At the instant of contact, he twisted, pulled in his legs and sprang upright. His body, face and hair streamed water. His mouth sucked in air, but his eyes were wide, unblinking and filled with maniacal intent. Clutched in his hand was a rock the size of a brick.

Greg had a fraction of a second to register this last detail before it descended.

THIRTY-NINE

He was floating on his back in the warm shallows. The sun was red on his closed eyelids, and he could hear the sounds of birds, far-off dogs and nearby laughter. This had always been one of his favourite things on the hottest days of summer, relaxing in the Cowichan River, with the frenetic world a comfortable distance away. He opened his eyes, turning lazily to watch the shore. His sister was playing in the shallows downstream, shadowed as usual by that Lucy kid from next door. His father had an easel set up on the grassy sward overlooking the water and was painting away, oblivious to the broiling sun. His mother, more sensibly, was reading under an umbrella.

But as he watched, something strange happened; his father threw down his paintbrush, marched down the bank and, fully clothed, walked into the river. Oblivious to the current, he kept on till his head vanished beneath the surface. Next, his mother dropped her book and did the same. Neither parent reappeared. Greg then saw that it was not his sister that little Lucy was playing with, but her own mother. Calmly, as if on cue, the pair walked hand in hand into the water and disappeared. Only then did the full horror of what was happening dawn upon him. He should be doing something about this, but found he couldn't move. Thick weeds clung to his legs. He jackknifed his body, plunging down to find what was restraining him: not weeds, but human hands. A ghastly array of clutching fingers, reaching up out of the gloom, attached themselves to his arms and head, dragging him inexorably down. His mum and dad hovered side by side, faces dark with condemnation. Little Lucy was there too, and her mother, but immersion had turned her into an old woman. Her eyes stared, in a manner he somehow remembered, and of all the phantoms, her expression was the ugliest. *Coward*, she croaked. *Murderer!* Then all were moving toward him, fingers reaching to rend him apart . . . and suddenly it all faded.

He opened his eyes to discover he was in big, white room, lying in a bed.

"Greg?"

He turned toward the soft voice. A young woman was sitting nearby, someone he didn't at first recognize—then, with a shock, he *did*. Instead of the drowned child of his nightmare, this was the grown-up Lucy. "Hello, Greg," she said gently. "Welcome back."

"Back?" His voice was a whisper, issuing from a throat that felt as dry as ancient parchment. Instantly, Lucy was up, proffering a container with a straw.

"Drink," she said. Then, answering his question. "Back from the dead, I guess."

The way he felt, that sounded about right. As he sipped from the straw, feeling the water soak the parchment, he realized he had no idea where he was or what had happened. So he asked, "Where am I?"

"Duncan Hospital. Mother's here, too."

"Your mother . . . ?" *Then* it all came back, the horrible litany of events, with such force that he could only stare numbly, until at last the—impossible—significance of her words penetrated. "Did you say—*here*? Your mother? But I thought—you told me . . ."

"She was dead? I know. I'm terribly sorry. After you set me free, I was nearly out of my mind, and I thought . . . But she was still alive. In a diabetic coma. By the time I'd realized that and given her a shot, you'd gone. I'm so sorry. If you hadn't come when you did, she certainly *would* have died."

"And you said she's here?"

Lucy almost laughed. "Yes, Greg, just down the hall."

"And she's going to be okay?"

"As well as she ever can be, yes. They say I can take her home in a couple of days."

He considered that for a moment. "How did I get here?"

Lucy gave a strange smile. "Well, the reason you're not in a much worse place, actually, is because you were shot."

Shot, yes, he remembered that now. "What do you mean?"

"By the time it got light, Mother and I had gone to the hospital. The police were still at the house, but they didn't know where you'd gone, or what had happened to Jay. No one thought to check the river. But then they heard shots coming from there, and everyone went running. By the time they found you, you were unconscious, face down at the edge of the water. Evidently, they got you out and gave you CPR only just in time."

Greg thought about that for a while. Now he could differentiate, through the general chorus of aches, the places at his shoulder and side where the bullets had struck. Not very successfully, he attempted a grin. "What didn't kill me saved my life, eh?"

"In effect, yes."

"Well, lucky me." Then another figure scuttled unpleasantly back to centre stage. "But I guess Jay got away?"

Lucy at last permitted herself a really big smile. "He probably would have. But when the police arrived, they saw the canoe—it was my dad's—they must have taken it from the shed—disappearing around the bend."

"And . . . ?"

"They radioed into town and set up an ambush."

"*And* . . . ?"

"Caught Jay just downstream of the old highway bridge."

"Well, hallelujah!" Greg lay quiet for a long time, savouring the thought of that.

"Don't you want to know about the money?"

So much good news had broken that Greg hadn't even thought of it. "Oh, yeah."

"It was all there. When they arrested Jay, they found it in the canoe. One of the cops, who didn't know about it, opened up the bag and nearly wet himself. That, and the cash Jay gave Trev, is all safely stored with the Duncan RCMP." She smiled, and he realized that she was holding one of his hands. "So you see—now that we haven't lost either you or Mum—we aren't in such bad shape at all."

"Little thanks to me, I'm afraid."

Lucy gave him that straight look that had always slightly intimidated him. "Nonsense," she said briskly. "You may have made some unwise decisions early on, but what you did in the end was kinder and braver than anyone had a right to expect. Your parents would have been proud of you. I know I am." She leaned down and kissed him, briefly but with purpose. "Now get some rest. I'll be back tomorrow."

After she was gone, Greg lay still, staring out the window. The pain in his body, though muted by drugs, was a background symphony. If not truly deserved, it felt appropriate, a reminder of the real world and of the extraordinary fortune that had allowed him to be here at all. Outside, the sky was sliding into night. He didn't know what day it was and didn't care. Soon he slept.

Ron Chudley is the author of three other TouchWood mysteries: *Old Bones* (2005), *Dark Resurrection* (2006) and *Stolen* (2007). He has written extensively for television (including *The Beachcombers*) and for the National Film Board of Canada, and has contributed dramas to CBC Radio's *Mystery, The Bush and the Salon* and CBC *Stage*. He lives with his wife, Karen, in Mill Bay, BC.

ISBN: 978-1-894898-59-1

ISBN: 978-1-894898-48-5

ISBN: 978-1-894898-33-1

"A moody psychological novel with a series of finely drawn characters."
—*The Globe and Mail*

"His characters are skilfully realized and the redemption is startling and tempting. A satisfying read from cover to cover."
—*Hamilton Spectator*